THE TIME FOR MONSTERS

AN ELDRITCH XENOMORPH MONSTER ROMANCE

J.M. KEEP

WITH

ALEXIS ABBOTT

PATHFORGERS PUBLISHING

Dedicated to all the survivors of the world's real horrors.
May your only monsters be those who mete our harsh justice.

PREFACE

Please note that this book contains multiple very serious triggers, including body horror, torture, and gore. There are brief mentions of child abuse, including emotional neglect and sexual abuse.

There are brief mentions of sexual violence not involving the MMC.

The romance is entirely consensual.

For a detailed list of triggers, please visit https://jmkeep.com

MAP

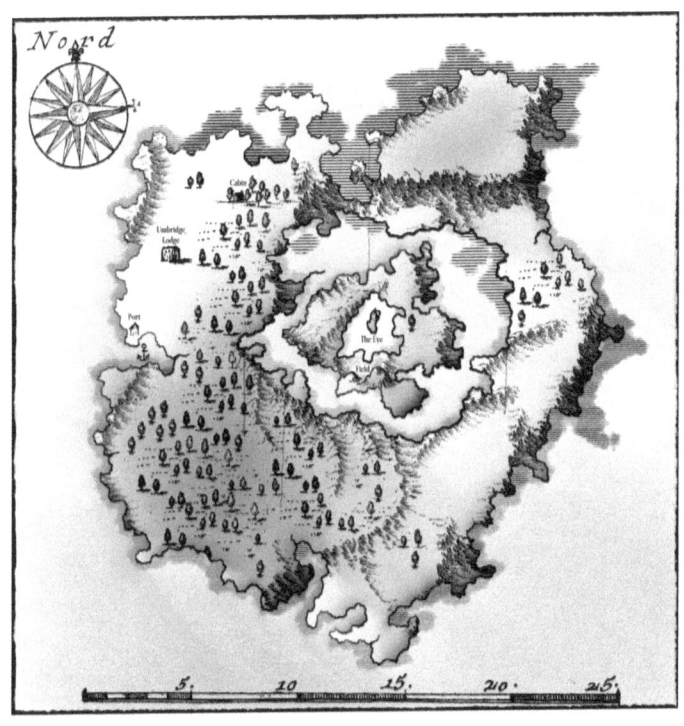

CHAPTER 1

"The old world is ~~dying~~ dead, and the new world ~~struggles to be~~ is born: now is the time of monsters."
—— **Antonio Gramsci**

Leet's apartment is always too cold. He's one of the few people in Neo-Victoria that has air conditioning, and while it's a pleasant reprieve from the oppressive heat, I shiver. His penthouse is higher even than the smog that blankets the city.

How did I get here?

I don't remember the walk.

Leet smiles, and I forget my confusion. He has a dimple on the left cheek, and his lips are peachy against his pale face.

"I never thought I'd get you alone."

It's an odd thing for him to say. We're always alone together. Before I can ask what he means, his hand is running through my dark hair, and his lips hover just an

1

inch away. He closes the distance, and my heart thuds like machinegun fire.

"You feel the same?" I ask, my usually dry voice dripping with emotion.

"Of course, Shayde. I've loved you for years." His skin is warm, a healthy flush contrasting against his black hair. His slender nose caresses mine. "Here. Let me help," he says, and I become aware of my nudity.

The room is dark, but we're illuminated by a strange halo of light. My back meets the bed. It's lumpy and hard. Cold.

It doesn't matter.

Leet feels the same way for me as I do for him.

That's what's important.

His body is heavier than I expect, given how slender he is, and the weight is bordering on unpleasant. His mouth finds mine before trailing down my jaw, down my neck. He teases his pierced tongue over one nipple, then the other. I press my fingers through his short hair and moan, encouraging his exploration of my body. There's a twig in his hair, and I pluck it out, tossing it aside.

Why is there a twig in his hair?

"I thought..."

What did I think? It's faded. My body is hot with lust, my mind foggy.

There's some emotion I don't understand, lurking just out of my grasp, and I force myself to relax. It's natural that I feel nervous. It's the first time that Leet has expressed these feelings for me. Of course I'd try to sabotage our moment.

He kisses down my stomach to my mons. I smile dreamily.

"Ow, careful," I hiss as something scratches my hip. I shift positions, but then it scratches me again, and I look down to see that his hands aren't touching me there. In fact, his hands aren't there at all. He's just a face, floating down between my thighs.

His smile spreads wide, wider, until his skull cracks in two and disappears into a cloud of viscera.

I wake up, sweating and clutching a pistol. This deep in the woods, the gloam is thick, even before the sun is set. I choke on fresh air, so rich in oxygen.

Reality returns slowly, and then all at once. My cybernetic implants are still on the fritz, but I never opted for the memory bank upgrade. That's all stored in my flesh and blood, so I have no trouble remembering what a shit show I'm in.

The forest is dense, swallowing all sound. I miss the noise of the city; the groan of metal as buildings sway in the wind, the street vendors. Hell, I'd take the shouting of the couple in the apartment next door over this.

I'd always wondered what nature was like. Grass and trees and water were all luxuries reserved for a better class of people than me, but this island is an alien prison that I'm not equipped to navigate.

There are no human noises. No conversations or grunts.

I strain my ears until I'm convinced I'm alone. I've never been so alone in all my life.

But there are others on the island. My best guess is that there are five hunters after me.

If I survive a week, I can go home free.

They'll never let that happen.

Not willingly.

If I'm going to get off this island, I need to kill the hunters before they kill me. Without my implants, that's a lot harder.

Harder. Not impossible.

I hope.

My sleep has been intermittent at best. Little bits of it here and there. Mostly during the day, as I'm harder to track at night. Also, the incessant swarms of black flies are unbearable during the day. They make travel awful. They make breathing awful.

They make existing awful.

In the open, the air becomes choked with them. What might have been lovely vistas were instead clouded with a blackish-grey filter of flies. The little parasites bite too. Small bites, but there's so many of them the size stops mattering.

On the second day, I found a trick for dealing with them. Tearing off one of my sleeves, I made a mask to hide my breath; they seem drawn by that. And then I caked my skin in mud.

I feel dirty—filthy, in fact—yet it's infinitely better than the sensation of those flies on my flesh every moment of the day. The flies don't bother the rich men who have made sport of me. They have some kind of bands they wear that keep the flies at bay.

They don't even have to suffer the choking pestilence as they hunt me down.

It all adds to the unmistakable feeling that I am the

alien here, though. Not just a city girl lost in the woods, but a creature from another world, being assaulted in every way imaginable by the local fauna.

It's been a couple of days since I last saw one of the hunters. When I first awoke at Umbridge Lodge, I knew I was in deep shit, but this? This is a level of fucked up beyond what my imagination could have conjured up.

The forest floor is hard and uneven, despite the mossy bed I found, and I groan as I push myself up. It's time to face the day.

Evening.

Whatever.

My stomach spasms. I haven't eaten in days; my body is wasting away. How can I tell what is poisonous? The forest is eerie in its stillness. Aside from the bugs, I rarely even hear a bird, let alone a mouse.

The chill of night settles in upon me. It's an unfamiliar sensation. I grew up in Neo-Victoria—NV—and it was always boiling hot and oppressive. The island must be very far north for it to still get cold. Was all ice at one point, but now it's lush and thick and terrifying.

I glance at a berry bush. I'd rejected them when I first found the hollowed-out stump that passed for my lodgings. Too risky. They're plentiful, so no animal has eaten them, but maybe that's just because there are no animals around.

Or maybe they're poison. I could end up doubled over in agony, moaning in irrepressible pain, dying over the course of days.

But now I'm too hungry. My body is crying out for sustenance. If I don't eat something, I won't have the energy to carry on.

At least if I starve to death, I'd be robbing the hunters of their prize.

It's been days of running, hiding... It's a miracle I can even stand. My vision is doubling, and I stare at the orange berries.

"What is this berry called?" I say aloud habitually.

My cybernetic implants tell me nothing. The same message about having no connection to the network flashes behind my eyelids.

They're not blackberries or raspberries, though they have the little cluster of pearls. They're smaller, orange. Growing close to the ground, they're as low as the moss.

I pick one, squeezing it between my thumb and forefinger. They are resilient. If I eat them, I could die. If I don't eat them, I will die.

My internal discussion is interrupted by the realization that I already am eating them.

Need won out.

The certainty of starvation beats the uncertainty of being poisoned.

My tattered clothes for city life. They make no sense here. The cool, hip boots I'd been so proud of back home are cumbersome and awkward in the wild woods. They're holding together, but the moisture is eating the foam.

My jeans are thick and rugged, at least. A small mercy, considering I usually wore leather shorts back home. They're good protection against the brush, but my arms are exposed, and my thin shirt offers no warmth or safety. It's the first time I've regretted the fact that I never wear a bra, because just that little bit of extra fabric would've been amazing.

Instead, I'm relying on mud to keep my base temperature up and stop the chill from creeping into me.

The damp, though. That's the worst. Aside from, you know, the fact that I'm being hunted for sport on an isolated island up north.

I've devoured a lot of the berries by now. If they're poisonous, I'm fucked.

A branch snaps. Sound is strange in the forest, diffused by leaves and bushes. If I can hear it at all, they're close. With my pistol in hand, I skulk along the mossy forest floor, past the low growing berries. My stomach growls in protest, but I've gorged enough.

Hiding doesn't work with these guys. The tech they're using hones in on me when I stay idle too long, so I keep moving in the same direction, away from the water.

Through the dying embers of the sunset behind me is the silhouette of a man with a big rifle, kitted out with many survival assistances.

His visor gives him night vision. Maybe thermal. These rich guys have all the latest tech that puts my inoperable implants to shame.

I move, cautious not to make noise. My body heats with adrenaline, my limbs trembling. Survival is all that matters.

A crack splits the air.

Beside me, a branch explodes into splinters as a bullet strikes it.

CHAPTER 2

The bullet narrowly misses me, and I leap, rolling through the moss.

My back against a log, I turn and fire a shot from my gun at the man. I have limited bullets, just what's in the gun, but I'm a crack shot—at least, I'd always been in VR—though I don't wait to see if I hit him.

So far, I'd fired three shots, and no signs of having hit anyone.

The bullets probably aren't even real.

They gave me the gun at the lodge, and I wouldn't put it past them to fill it with blanks, just to fuck with me.

My muscles burn as I sprint through the woods, away from the hunter. My muscles ache for not just berries, but protein.

Another shot resonates through the woods.

No idea how close it is.

My lungs are on fire. I inhale a cloud of bugs.

That'll be all the protein I can get for now, so I try not to spit them out. Their wings twitch in my saliva and I gag.

Men shout behind me, yipping. They're so happy. It's a game to them.

They have network communications, and there's no need for them to be yelling and hollering. But they do it anyway, because they think it's just a matter of time before I'm taken out. It's their vacation, hunting girls on a desert island.

Their bullets are real. The Umbridge Lodge, where I woke up a few days ago, was filled with trophies.

Don't think about those.

I'm pushing my body past limits I thought I had as I run. Some of the bristly evergreen branches tear at my skin, tangle and tear at my hair, but I can't stop or waste time.

I just gotta keep going.

Another shot cracks through the dark air, the sun dying entirely as I keep going. It's pitch black now, and I'm at risk of hurting myself by running through the wilderness blindly. Grey clouds diffuse the moon, and the canopy of green encases me.

A flicker, a momentary glimpse.

A light in the distance.

I emerge from the treeline, trying to catch sight of it again. I've been moving away from the Lodge for days. It can't be theirs. I'm in the open air, staring out at the vast darkness, seeking that little ray of hope.

Another gunshot. I sprint ahead.

Only thing is, there's no land between me and what I saw.

I plunge into inky black water. My body stiffens in shock, the freezing cold sensation burning my flesh. My jeans tear on some rocks on the shore. An icy hell envelops me. My limbs flail as I search for the surface.

I emerge and gasp for air.

A gunshot rings out.

I plunge down again.

No way but onward. Swim. Keep my head below water as much as possible.

Easier said than done.

Fear and adrenaline crash within me, my motions frantic and uncoordinated. I've never been a strong swimmer, and my aching muscles don't find swimming any easier than running was.

Not to mention the water is so cold it hurts.

Ironic that it feels like my body is on fire as ice chills my veins.

I won't last long in the water, but fuck, I have a half dozen guys hunting me for sport. My odds have never been great, and at least drowning would steal any triumph they might feel.

Plus, I'd avoid whatever indignities they'd wanna perform on me post-mortem.

What I saw in their depraved lodge horrifies me.

Upon the walls of that posh hunter's getaway were antlered deer and moose heads. Bears. Lynxes. Coyotes. Wolves.

But more horrifying things adorned the place as well.

I'd seen the human skulls, arranged in patterns, as if a part of some sick art project. I hurled my guts out all over the wood flooring when I saw the human body. Horror was etched in the man's face forever, locking him in time and place when he was killed. His flesh was covered in cuts and bruises, lovingly preserved and displayed for all time.

They'd tortured him before he finally was killed.

"It's just a wax replica," the masked man had told me in the most insincere voice imaginable.

He didn't expect me to believe it, just like he didn't expect me to believe that I can survive a week here.

Where is the damn shore?!

I keep swimming. Past the point of no return. I swim past the surety of the shore behind me. There's nothing left to turn back to. I just kept swimming, bobbing my head above water to gulp air.

Every time I flag, or slow down, there's a shot. A bullet hitting the water, zipping past me.

My limbs sting. I keep going. And going.

Did I pass out?

Time blurs. I don't remember finding shore, but the eddies push me forward until something solid is beneath my knees. I clamour forward, crawling on hands and knees like the first mammal to walk on land.

The cloud cover has broken. The moon and stars hang overhead. It's so beautiful I could cry, and I wish I had the luxury to bask in the majesty of nature. My gaze lowers, and I stare at the black lake I just crossed.

It arcs to either side, encompassing the land I now stand on.

Looking back from where I came, I see nothing. But I can't afford to linger. I get up and crawl inland. More trees. Shelter. I rush to its embrace as another bullet cracks through the night air.

My flesh stings, and I push on. The woods close in around me, and finally things go still. Cold water drips from my t-shirt, my thighs chafing from my jeans. I lean against a thick tree, touching the point in my side where my skin is raw.

I can't go any further. I need a breather. I need a break.

But even my rest is polluted by them all. The memories, the resentment, about how I ended up here flooding back.

Leet.

That fucker.

I *trusted* him.

No, worse than that. I thought he was a person with a conscience. We were both hackers, and I was under the impression that we were working towards a noble goal. I hadn't liked anyone except him in years. I thought I knew him.

When I found out who he was working for, of *course* I told him.

Then I woke up in Umbridge Lodge, being told the rules of the game.

He sold me out, and when I see him again, I'm going to...

I'm too tired for all this rage. There'll be time to concoct a fitting revenge plot later. For now, I need to survive.

I push myself back to my feet and head further inland. Hopefully this island is an escape. From what little I know of those men hunting me, they aren't the type to come swimming after me. They'll insist on finding a boat to make the passage.

So, at the very least, I bought myself time to—
The world spins.
My vision doubles.
The wound isn't even that...

CHAPTER 3

"There are men several feet taller than you with balls smaller than yours, Shayde."

Leet and I share a bottle of wine, relaxing in his luxury apartment. I've fallen for him, not fast, but over the course of several years of friendship. I catch his dimples and my heart thuds over itself. His compliments are so rare, and I squeal with excitement internally.

Externally, I laugh, trying to act like the cool girl.

"It's just what anyone would do, if they had this access to Umbridge & Sons." We recline in the loft of his spacious condo. He has more furniture than the last time I was here. I don't ask about his money, but we aren't in the same social class anymore. At least we can talk here, unlike my dingy apartment. He has a multi-level air-gapping system installed to keep him safe from other hackers, and all spying eyes are disabled.

"No, Shayde. It's not. You're special. This is dangerous. Are you sure you want to do this?"

He's so handsome. Not in a traditional way, I guess. His

dark hair is sleek and swept black, his eyes intense and glinting with brilliance.

He's a sharp dresser, too, always wearing some bespoke outfit that stands out from the crowd. If he weren't such a nerd like me, I'd swear he was a fashion model. He's too lanky to be considered traditionally attractive, tall, a little bit unusual. I'm smitten.

I have no idea how he feels about me. It's great that he's not a lecherous pervert like most male hackers I've met, but he's almost too respectful of me.

"Infiltrate an arms dealer, disrupting the flow of weapons across the globe? Rob them blind so they can't drop another fucking nuke on a bunch of innocence civilians? Of *course* I want to do this, Leet. What kind of person would I be if I didn't?"

His dimple deepens, and I drift closer into his personal bubble. His body heat warms me up. While I like the break from the heat that his air-conditioned penthouse provides, my skin prickles with goosebumps.

"You'll be taking on the riskiest part, though, Shayde. I'll just be handling the financial side of things, safe and sound from my HQ. You'll be the one breaking into the warehouse."

"I know. But this might be our only chance to disrupt the war machine. No matter what happens to me, it'll be worth it if we can pull this off. Besides, to live is to approach death gradually. I can't keep doing this slow march."

He shakes his head, and the respect in his gaze is addictive. Our shared passion for a better world unites us.

"How the hell did you get so brave?"

I'm not brave, but I like that Leet thinks I am. He

doesn't expect an answer. He knows I don't like talking about myself or my past.

"Umbridge & Sons think they're untouchable. Together, we can bring them to their knees. And besides, no one will miss me if..."

If something happens. If I'm caught, thrown in a cell to rot. Killed in the warehouse. My parents abandoned me after I hacked my school network and exposed widespread grade tampering to favour rich kids. They blamed me for getting expelled from the prestigious Owasis Prep School they fought to get me into.

My girlfriend, Vivian, said she'd stay with me. After all we'd been through, I'd believed her. I was the one she always relied on once she came out, after she started to transition. Her light burned so bright, and I thought we'd be together forever.

After a few weeks, she'd moved on and broke my heart.

My cousin Aimi offered me a place to stay in Kyoto. She died before I could get there.

I have no one.

Leet reaches out and brushes some of my hair around the shell of my ear. My heart lodges in my throat.

"I'll miss you," he says in a deeper, more seductive voice, his eyes sweeping over me.

"We should make the most of this moment. There's no telling how this operation will go down. As good as we are, the company's got big assets. Clever people who work for them, aside from me."

The gap between us closes. Lust prickles beneath my skin, but there's something entwined with it. Hot rage accompanies it, but that doesn't make sense.

I've never been mad at Leet.

He's always been there for me. He was the one who helped me get my life back on track after the asylum.

I haven't talked to my parents in the better part of a decade, and Leet fills that gaping hole in my heart that I pretend isn't there.

"I think I'm falling in love with you," I murmur.

He cups my jaw and caresses along my cheek with his thumb. His skin is cold and firm, like marble.

This isn't real. It's a memory.

A bittersweet memory.

It's comforting to lose myself in it. To pretend this is reality. I don't fight it as he shifts in closer on that posh, expensive sofa of his, and our faces drift closer together.

"Teach me what love is."

Something feels off.

That isn't what he's supposed to say.

He leans in and kisses me, our lips glancing. "Is this love?" he asks in a breathy voice. His hard, tall form presses into me tighter. The kisses grow frenzied, assertive.

For a while, I'd wondered if Leet was gay, or asexual, maybe. Or, yeah, maybe he just thought of me as a friend, a peer. I was happy he thought of me at all, and being his friend was almost as good as being his lover.

These kisses contain all the things I've been longing for.

I part my lips, my hand on his leg as I lean in towards him, matching his passion. I've fantasized about this, and this is all my dreams coming true.

It's unsettling the way he responds to my desires with such speed. Every time he gets too aggressive, he backs off. When I want more, he's back. His hands move just where I want them, his nimble fingers unfastening the buckles on my top.

He takes the lead, but he follows my unspoken directions with ease.

The room had grown dark behind him while we'd been making out. He peels back my top and takes hold of a breast, caressing it.

"I want you," he says, and his eyes are like dark pools now in the dim light. "I'm glad for all the circumstances that brought you here, to this moment. To me."

I melt.

Those words. Ah fuck, they just totally unravel me, get through to my barbed wire heart. I'm trembling and there's a hot warmth behind my eyes. I deny myself that childish impulse and kiss him hard on the mouth, hungry to swallow those words. To absorb them into me, and my consciousness. To make them a part of who I am.

Our mouths are locked together, tongues entwined. And my hands move to his chest, feeling that hard physique through his vest and shirt, before beginning to unbutton and remove them.

This isn't a memory.

It's changed, but it's pleasantly different. Better. So much better.

His cool hands slide along my body, feeling me up, marvelling over my flesh as he looms over me.

"Shayde..."

He says my name with such poignancy and desire. It's hunger laced with longing greater than anything I'd ever heard before. As if he were starved for human contact, and then found me, surpassing all desires and expectations.

His hands are working open his belt and pants, and I look at him, watching that unveiling of his manhood.

Leet and I had fucked in the actual moment, but in this memory it's more passionate. Love radiates out from him. His cock spills out, already engorged.

"I need you," he says.

His face is a little off. His familiar dark eyes seem to cry tears of ink. The ceiling of the room beyond him breathes. Great roots pulse like veins. Concrete gives way to life.

Don't pay attention to that. I'm just trying to ruin the moment like I always do, shying away from the intimacy that I desperately crave.

His hips angle down, his manhood pressed to my slit.

"I need you," I breathe back, my mouth pressing against his as his body weighs down on me. "Never leave me. Promise you'll never leave me."

I haven't even finished the words when a rumble passes through me, through the ground, dark and rolling.

"I promise."

It feels so good to have not just his physical presence and desire, but his devotion. It's euphoric. He penetrates me and I moan. He's big and filling, stretching me wide.

"I want to know what it's really like."

There's a strange reverberation in his voice, an echo. His hips pump to the perfect tempo, at the perfect angle. He knows my body better than I do. His pace rises gradually, and I writhe beneath him in bliss.

I never want this dream to end.

"Come..." he bids me. I'm already perched at the edge of orgasm. So close to giving him what he wants.

"Come to me."

To me?

That's a strange thing to say. He's already inside me. I'm as close to him as can possibly be, and the pleasure is mounting higher and higher. I wrap my arms around his back, surprised by how large he feels.

"Find the centre of the eye…"

I don't understand. My body is buckling under the intensity. I force my eyes open to catch his gaze—maybe he wants more eye contact?—but everything is wrong.

The walls lined with throbbing, vein-like tubes pulsate and ooze, as if we're inside some big heart of a blackened demon. And Leet…

Leet's eyes are still wrong, but now that ink has begun to consume him. His whole being is black now, instead of the pale flesh I knew. His powerful hands grip me tighter, the feeling of long sharp claws glancing my flesh.

He's not Leet. Not the Leet I knew. Not in action or looks. And there, perched on the edge of orgasm, I scream and scream until I awake on the forest floor.

I'm sticky with sweat and it reminds me of the ooze. My inner thighs are wet beneath my jeans, and I worry I pissed myself, but the reality is worse. Arousal wafts in the air, and that dream is so vivid, even as I suck in cold air, my frantic eyes searching for something I can't see. Something no one *should* see.

The monster of my dreams.

CHAPTER 4

I'm uncertain if my scream was out loud or not, but I can't take the chance it was. I have to get moving. When I try to stand, I remember the splitting pain in my... no. The bullet had come close, but on examination, I have no wound. A scrape from the rocks when I hit the water, but the bullet missed.

There's no external reason for me to have passed out like that.

Maybe there's a gas? A drug? But that would go into the atmosphere. It'd be hella expensive to drug me like that. The berries? My stomach feels fine, though I suppose it's a possibility they were psychoactive. The hunger and fear would give me a bad trip.

That's all it was.

A terrible trip.

I try to push the memory of the inky monster, the throbbing walls, out of my mind.

A ridge juts up out of the forest. I have to climb it to

make progress. It'll make me easier to see, but it'll also give me a moment's advantage to see if they're coming too.

With little other choice, I just begin to climb and climb. Grasping hold of branches for support as I find footholds in the mossy dirt. The route is not direct. No straight lines here. Even a zigzag would feel direct by comparison.

I reach a point where I'm dangling with no ledge, holding into thick branches coming out of the dirt and rock wall. I have to will myself not to look down as my feet either dangle or scrape against the mossy stone faces.

My heart is racing, the tension high; I must be exposed like this. If one of those hunters sees me, he could pick me off a mile away with his rifle.

But thinking about that now is doing nothing more than spiking my anxiety. I just gotta move... move again. And again.

Until finally I can reach over and find some placement for my foot once more. I have to lean towards it, unsure if the branch I'm holding onto won't give. Unsure if the footing I've found is secure. There are no certainties, and at this point there's about a twenty-foot drop.

A leap of faith it is then.

Faith for the faithless, I throw myself into it.

The dirt gives, sinking down.

My heart races. It's too late now. I either keep going and hope it doesn't give way more, or I topple to my doom anyhow.

The dirt falls away in clumps, but I try to throw myself forward, and despite the sheer madness of it, it works! I land face down atop the ridge, rocks and dirt tumbling down the cliff behind me.

I break into a manic fit of laughter.

I could kiss the ground, but revelling is a luxury I can't afford. Still, I'm giddy as I push myself up to my feet, eager to get as much distance between me and the cliff face as I can. Maybe there's a cave or some place that could pass for shelter so I can catch my breath, get my bearings.

Hell, maybe there's some food here. Can you eat moss? I don't think so.

I pause when I see some bush near the ledge, and I use that to creep back towards it. Peering through and down, I get a better vantage point of where I'd come from.

There is the lake I'd swam across. Beyond that is the land I'd spent the last week hiding in. In the far distance is another lake.

An island within an island.

A prison within a prison.

I've fled my pursuers, falling deeper into a geographic trap than ever.

It could have been beautiful. The green is so bright it almost aches, even in the darkness. Silver waves lap against the rugged shore. The satellites are hunks of metal floating in orbit, but the stars are brighter than I'd ever imagined. Shapes, the constellations, were always just something taught me in school. Hypothetical things sparkling in the night sky.

I'd never seen them in person until I got here.

The hunters won't even allow me the pleasure of studying them. They're on the far shore, preparing a boat.

I knew they'd be too wimpy to swim across as I had. They'd let the night get away from them as they sought a cozy answer. Dawn is breaking, and I swat away a cloud of flies. There aren't as many here, at least, but I unconsciously scratch at my arm and know I need protection.

I'd gotten much needed rest, whether I wanted to or not, but now I have to move. I grab some dirt, rubbing it on my ruddy skin, covering as much of my exposed flesh as I can. My stomach rumbles again, though 'rumble' doesn't quite describe the sensation. It's a gaping maw of unfathomable, endless hunger that sits deep within me, threatening to consume me whole if I don't fill it, and fill it adequately this time.

The berries had bought me some energy and time, but I'm wasting away. You can't argue with results, but the survivalist-fleeing-for-your-life diet I'm on isn't one I'd recommend.

Covered in the natural debris of nature, I resume the journey. This ridge is overshadowed by another, rockier one. I find some gaps in it and head up more.

This must be the mountain looking area I'd seen in the distance when I'd first set out.

God, I hope it's not as tall as a mountain.

My hands hurt from all the bare grasping of rocks before I'm halfway up. My limbs cry out for sustenance and I press on, this time avoiding catastrophe. Sharp peeks jut upwards, a rocky crevice sliced through it, revealing the other side. My chest heaves as I squeeze through the mossy rock walls.

The wind sings as it moves through it, the occasional rock or pebble providing some percussion. The sound is hypnotic, and despite my exhaustion, I smile.

It's stolen away as I stand on a natural perch, staring

down into the crater. A chill travels my spine and my blood runs cold.

There is a ring of rock walls overshadowing the centre of the island, cupping another lake. The dark ring forms the iris, and within it lays another land mass. The pupil of the eye.

Dreams don't come true.

Neither do nightmares.

But this is just as Leet described it. The shimmering blue waters surrounded by stone grey rocks lined with mossy veins. A dark little island.

What fucking dark force of nature occurred to make this strange, crater-like 'eye' of the island within an island within an island, within an island?

Do I want to know?

My impulse is to ask my implants to look it up. But I remember in time they won't help me. Not in the least. The decision of what to do next is all mine.

CHAPTER 5

D o I go towards the eye? That place the dream realm I don't believe in sent me a grisly vision of?

Or do I go back?

Back into the hands of those who wish to murder me...

Simply murder, if I'm lucky.

Maybe I could sit here, wait for them to get to the foot of the mountain. I could pick them off as if I'm a hotshot sniper instead of a girl who learned to shoot at the arcade in VR.

No.

As much as these men deserve to be killed, I'm not like them. How can I possible shoot another person, even if they deserve to be shot? The pistol they gave me isn't something I can rely on, besides my own capacity to kill. I've never known rich guys to play fair. They wouldn't even know what fair was if it hit them in the mouth.

It's all a rationalization to cover for the *pull* the eye has on me. A magnet drawing me in.

That's too fucked up to even reckon with.

Food. Food first.

I descend into the lush valley. This leg of the journey is easier. This side is a gradual slope rather than a sharp cliff, and the trees aren't as dense. The moss and branches growing out complicate things, but they shouldn't be a prob—

I trip on some branch and go tumbling. The fucking ground is more treacherous than I ever imagined! Or else, my exhaustion and fatigue are just making me extra susceptible.

Branches scrape at my flesh as I roll, tearing at my clothes. Patches of thick moss are so soft they prevent damage, but I bounce off them, which sets me to rolling again.

I try to grab onto some branches, but they tear at my hand and they do nothing to slow my descent.

A patch of sharp rocks juts out ahead. If I hit them, that's it. I grasp wildly, trying to find something solid, but find nothing. The sun is rising over the cliffs and it burns my eyes with the intensity.

Rocky death approaches, and I flip onto my back. Lifting my heels, I stab them into the ground just as I find a thick root. Coarse bark rips my palms, blood gushing to the surface. I scrape over jagged rocks, my t-shirt tearing beneath me.

The root is torn from my grasp, and while I've slowed my movement, I still plummet down.

Thick moss spreads beneath me, and I grab hold of the edge with burning, bleeding hands. It peels away from the rock before it hitches. My head is half a foot away from being split open on a sharp-edged rock.

But as I lay there, catching my breath, I notice that it's not moss beneath me. It's another big patch of low berries that rises just above the moss. They have the same clustered look of the berries I ate the day before, except the colours are more bright and varied.

Bright berries are less deadly, right? Since they attract birds?

I have no fucking idea, and I don't care. I gather a handful of them and only then exercise some caution by trying one first. It's a little tart, but not too bitter. I wait a minute, then a minute longer, and since I don't double over in pain, the rest of the handful is tossed into my mouth and I'm gorging myself.

I'm a starving, injured woman laying amid a field of bounty. That's it, that's what's happening, I will not question it anymore than that.

I eat and eat and eat for what feels like hours. Still, there are endless more to be had. My shirt is stained red, and I'm sure my lips and cheeks match.

The moss seems higher now. It sways, a living sea of tall, fuzzy grass. I giggle, reaching out and brush my palms across the top of them, letting them tickle me. Warm light bathes the bowl of the cratered island, and the flora comes alive.

The moss and plants rise, dancing in the sun. I sink back into it, smiling at its embrace. Nature welcomes me into it, and I think back on my dream after eating the first berries. The comforting, alternate version of what had happened between Leet and I.

In my dream we made love.

In reality, Leet had fucked me.

We'd fucked.

It was fast. Hard. He was ravenous. There was no love in it.

I made excuses for him. He was just over-eager in his want of me. He'd fucked me too hard by mistake. I warned him I wasn't on birth control and he'd cum inside me, anyway.

I'd forgiven him, even though he never asked for it.

"Don't worry, Shayde." His smile was cocky, filled with an unearned confidence. "None of that is gonna matter after tomorrow."

I was a love-struck fool, convinced he meant that once we took down the arms dealer, we'd have enough money to settle down together. We could raise a family in peace, knowing we've earned that.

I can see the truth in all things. The truth in the past.

I walk through the meadow of squirming plant life, so unearthly, the colours of that valley taking on a strange, almost purple-ish hue, and I know.

Leet had used me.

He'd fucked me too hard because he knew I was a toy he wouldn't get to use again.

He wasn't worried about breaking me. He wasn't worried about ruining our friendship, or a chance for a relationship. That night, he wanted to fuck a living dead girl.

Despite what the man in the Lodge said, they're never going to let me go back to Neo-Victoria. What, and risk me exposing their sick little hunting trips?

Leet knew that after he sold me out, I'd never come back alive.

Rage is overshadowed by grief, and humiliation, and then it bounces right back to anger. My most familiar companion.

I just never thought I could reserve such a deep and boiling well of it for Leet, the man I thought I loved. Maybe I did love. Acknowledging that now feels shitty, though, and everything already feels too shitty for me to add more to the pile.

I sway as I stare down at the breathing plants, the coarse brush so much higher than I remembered. Was it always up to my knees? No. And it wasn't always that colour. A colour I'm not sure exists, or at least, isn't one humans can usually see.

I move through an ocean of life, becoming part of it. Writhing stalks of plant life coil around my feet, but they don't hold me back. I continue, and I gain greater and greater awareness as I go.

This is not an ocean full of life. It is one life. Singular. A great seething mass of life that resonates with my own hurt and rage.

It, too, had been hurt. Betrayed. Banished.

How I can communicate with such an incompatible life as plants, I can't say. Except that it's the emotional resonance. That rage at betrayal courses through it and me until we are one. I am not swimming through a school of fish; I am becoming a member of the school.

My skin hums and sings with the beautiful melody of hate.

Yes, I hate Leet now.

Hate him for what he did to me.

Hate him for who he is. A self-serving hypocrite, who would rain down death and murder on untold others, just to line his own pockets. Just to protect his own ass.

I have been walking for ages, and yet it feels like no time at all. Leet stands amid the sea of stalks. He's oozing black again in the orange light of the setting sun.

His mouth moves, but I hear nothing. The communication I have with this life all around me is not in words. It is emotion. Raw emotion only. We cannot share words, for our languages are too different. But we can share in rage. In hate.

I move towards the struggling, lethargic figure of Leet, and as I near him, from out of the sea of plant life, an old, hardened root is passed to me. It is dead, it's no longer part of the mass, and hasn't been for an age. Embedded at the end is a weighty, black rock that shimmers obsidian in the dying light.

There's just one thing to do.

The oozing Leet struggles against the same stalks that run up my legs, only they hinder him. They keep him pinned. And while I can't hear his words, I can read in his face, on his lips, that fear, that desperation. That pleading.

My dream, the foreboding feeling it gave me, has no place here. It's almost silly that I thought it was terrifying at the time, because this pure acceptance of who I am and what I feel is the most peaceful moment of my life. Ironic since rage and peace sound like opposites, but shared rage, this deep connection, gives me a home I've always longed for.

The root is heavy in my hand, but it's an extension of

myself, so lifting it is easy. Bringing it down is a nearly orgasmic release.

I watch what happens in slow motion. The beautiful arc of my arm, the old, hardened root, the obsidian stone. The crunch of bone, the splatter of blood. Again and again, it goes on like some ancient rhythm that matches the beat of my heart.

I bludgeon this inky black Leet, again and again. I unleash my rage; I bestow upon him justice.

No, better than justice.

Vengeance.

And my arm never grows tired, thanks to the support of the tendrils that had gone from wrapping around my ankles and calves, all the way to my arms. My muscles are never sore or weary, I just keep beating on him.

Again.

And again.

And again.

CHAPTER 6

This is another dream, and I stand in it, lucid and aware.

The Leet I see is not him.

That handsome face is bereft of his consciousness.

"You're almost there," he says, with a voice that would never have belonged to the Leet I knew. With a warm, caring smile Leet never could muster. Because he never did care, nor did he care enough to fake it. I had been a sucker. A sucker for love. A schoolgirl's crush, past its prime.

No, the figure I am talking to now is a manifestation of the living mass that had helped me. That had given me that taste of vengeance.

The man I'd beaten to a black mass in my drugged-waking state was not Leet. It was an appetizer. An amuse-bouche. A little taste.

A promise.

An intoxicating promise.

It awakened something in me I never wanted to acknowledge, never wanted to indulge.

I've always been afraid of my anger, that it would become so big that it would envelop me whole. After Aimi died, I did a stint in a mental hospital, and I learned how to hide my rage. Keep it tucked away, deep inside me.

When I close my eyes, I can see her community. Hear her pride as she told me about her garden. Then, inevitably, the smiling faces of her neighbours distort, melting away as the mental image always returns to the man responsible.

His cruel face has haunted me for a decade, and I was so close to cutting off the supply of weapons he received from Umbridge & Sons.

The company had started as a doomsday prepper company in the early twenty-first century after some terrorist attack in old New York. They started arming white nationalists not long after that, and as wars broke out, their power and influence grew. Private military contractors and mercenaries loved the subtle references to 1488 and other Nazi dog-whistle shit. Umbridge & Sons loved pretending they were innocent Americans who just loved a particular amendment.

After the United States fell, their power was clenched. There's no longer any need for them to hide who and what they are. No one has been able to touch them.

I was supposed to go down in history as the hacker who took them down.

There never was a name for the anger I felt at that, nor for the burning sensation I got whenever I remembered how easily my parents abandoned me, my friends dropped me.

I was never anything to anyone.

But I'm *everything* to this Leet.

"Come to the Eye..." it bids me with a curl of its long fingers, just like Leet's. Only the more he curls them, the more they look like those swaying stalks and fronds. And behind him I see it. That dark centre, nested island. Obsidian slabs stacked in a strange sculpture, resting in on each other as a tent.

"Then we can be free..." it promises.

Free.

If anyone else, anything else, had promised me that, I'd have scoffed. Freedom is just a thing they tell you is possible with enough money. A way to string you along as you abandon all morals and values until you realize you've sacrificed all you are for a slightly bigger apartment and a full fridge.

It's bullshit.

Except this time, it isn't.

I'm on an island within an island, a prison within a prison, being hunted by rich and powerful men like I'm game. Freedom should feel like even more of an illusion now, but this isn't the world I know.

Maybe here, there is something *like* freedom.

"What do you want?" I ask it.

Part of me already knows.

The familiar, handsome face grins. Only the grin keeps growing and growing, and growing, until the top of Leet's head is opening up, revealing rows of ominous fangs.

CHAPTER 7

I awake with a startle, gasping in air. It's evening again. The sky is clear; the moon is bright. Moss and grass —or it looks like grass—is all around me. The stalks and fronds are no longer swaying.

I'm in a wild, still field, and everything is normal.

It was all a dream.

A hallucinogenic induced dream.

I bring a hand up to push back some stray dark hair, but it's holding something heavy. My grip releases. My hand is black in the moonlight, as if stained by ink.

No. Oh no.

My heart rate rises and I scramble to stand up. There's a slick sound as my hand lands in something squishy. Wet. Fleshy.

My eyes have adjusted to the dark fast. The silvery light illuminates a body in camo hunting gear.

His skull is caved in, his face beaten off. The puddle of gore is still fresh, but it no longer resembles a person. I stumble back, dry heaving as my stomach churns. Nothing comes up, not even the acid that's burning inside me.

I killed someone.

Someone who deserved it.

My hands dig into the reeds, and they caress my palm. It soothes me as I sob and gasp for air. Guilt gives way to something else. Relief, and then joy. For once, an innocent woman survived against a dangerous man, and I'm horrified to feel my lips twitch in desire to smile. It's wrong to enjoy this, and I resist the urge.

Get my bearings.

That's what I need to focus on.

A breeze rustles the surrounding fronds, only I feel no breeze at all. Everything is dead still. Whatever moves them comes from below. While the silvery moonlight illuminates the valley for me, the distance is drenched in shadow. Ridges outline a crater, and housed in the middle of it is another island.

The eye.

Sheer dumb luck won't save me forever. Escaping this place means turning back towards the lodge and my pursuers.

But the site from my dreams beckons me. It's so close. I can make the last swim, at night, across that inky black pond, to the inner island.

I've never been a girl that favours random fate. In school, I was always the logical one, the one with a plan.

This is a shit plan, but it's all I have.

More than that, I have a deep need to *know*. To understand. Maybe this is all some random hallucination, but I have a feeling it's not, and so what is it?

Faced with taking my chances with a group of rich, tricked out hunters, and the dark vision of my dreams... I choose my dreams.

The field is so deathly still. Not a single sound.

The quiet draws on so long that I take for granted I'm alone. Safe.

When the antlered deer jumps out of its tall grass hideaway, I'm shocked into a scream.

We observe each other in stunned silence until it scuffs a hoof. Its gleaming, fanned antlers lower in my direction. My pistol is waterlogged and not much of a match against a deer, but I don't have a choice.

It charges.

I pull the trigger.

Nothing.

I pull again. And again.

The sound is loud, amplified by the natural crater that surrounds me. As the bullets strike the deer, the animal doesn't flinch. It's all for show. I might as well be shooting off flares to highlight my location.

I am defenseless against this mighty creature as it charges towards me, ready to gore me.

I fall to the ground, curling my hands over my head as if that'd save me. My fate is sealed. I had no idea how massive deer were. They always looked so beautiful and harmless in the storybooks. Its hooves echo as he descends upon me.

The deer stumbles. Some unseen force has put its charge off centre. I scramble backwards as it plants headfirst into the ground, rending furrows in the moss and dirt with its antlers.

The entire valley is alive. This time, the hallucinogenic

berries aren't there to be blamed for any of it. The rustling of stalks and fronds bristling in anger are on my behalf.

Time pauses.

Everything settles, but for a light, tremulous sensation that I feel on an instinctive level more than experience with my senses.

I risk approaching the animal. In the dark, there's only so much I can make out from a safe distance. The deer is ensnared in... something. But all I see are the fronds, the stalks, the roots.

This is all new to me. There are no real animals in NV other than the rats and racoons and the odd pigeon. Nothing as large as this wild animal. How can I tell if this poor animal is dead? Do deer feign death when scared? If it is dead, I could theoretically skin it and eat it. I'd be full for a month, but how the fuck would I do that? I don't have a knife.

So, I just stare at it in confusion and wonder, this beautiful, dangerous creature. This wild thing. I feel a kinship with it, despite how different from me it is, but on this island, we're both just prey.

I take a chance and kneel a few feet away lest it bucks. One knock to the head and I'd be as good as dead.

I'm not sure why. Curiosity, maybe. Respect. Even to myself, I am an enigma. I just want to be close to it.

Their motions are subtle. I kneel, catching my breath, and watch as the reeds that were loosely twined about it gradually tighten, sinking into its fur.

The deer bucks, and resumes a more frenzied resistance, and I have to back away for safety's sake. But it keeps up its struggle, as the very valley works to protect me from it.

"It's only frightened," I say. My words are wasted; I am all alone.

Just the still air, the rustling of the brush coming from below rather than above. It's unsettling and comforting, all at once.

We can communicate, the entity and I, but not like this. When I'm awake, words mean nothing. It was only with a tummy full of hallucinogenic berries that we could share emotions.

The deer remains caught, bucking wildly.

In the absence of language, the being can only commit itself to protecting me.

I know that now.

Reaching the shore of the pond, glinting stonework juts ahead. The land doesn't so much end, as it melts into wet reeds and boggy matter until finally I am up to my knees in the murky water.

The reeds in the water caress my body like a tender lover.

Its temperature is that of a womb. The liquid is an extension of me, and I am weightless in it. Not just physically, but something deeper. A return to something I can't remember with my conscious mind, but that my body knows intimately.

For the first time since waking on this fucking hunting ground, I sense peace, close at hand.

Earlier that day, one of the hunters had nearly caught me, but it had protected me. Helped me protect myself.

Now I go to it.

Seek it out.

Seek out its comfort and protection.

My kindred spirit, mired in rage and lust for vengeance.

As I paw my way up onto the shore, the swim much shorter than the last lake I crossed, I'm panting. The reeds had made things so much easier, the water a pleasing temperature unlike the icy chill of the last.

My clothes soaked, I crawl up onto that island, and it strikes me... the distinct lack of sound there. The flies that had plagued me on the first days of the hunt were a distant memory now. Nothing moves but the beckoning sway of the stalks and fronds.

I finally force myself up onto my feet, my soaking clothes a nuisance as I move in towards the centre of the island.

CHAPTER 8

I'm being beckoned to a certain point by recollection of a repetitious dream. One of the countless visions I can't remember, but which has played out thousands of times during my sleep.

The stones are bigger than I imagined. They tower over me as a gate; a triangular hole with a dark middle, beyond which lies my fate. I feel it, without words.

This is messed up. I'm so calm, and that's upsetting, because there's something inhuman in there. Something we don't have words or names for. Something I should be fucking running away from, but my kind—humans—have pushed me to the brink.

I'm looking for a fucking *monster* because that's better than the other people on this island. At least whatever is in this cave wants to protect me, in its own way.

So I enter, knowing that it might be the last thing I do.

Knowing that it won't be even close to the last thing I do.

Minutes drag into hours as I descend beneath the

surface of the earth. The entrance was roughly hewn by nature, but this isn't a natural cavern. It widens, carved and hollowed out by thinking hands. The coarse edges of rock are chiselled away as I follow the path down; a gateway to the Underworld.

Thin roots find the cracks in the old stone, reaching ever upwards. Life persevering against the odds. A strange, unknown sort of life, but life no less.

When I touch them, I feel a tingle of familiarity.

Whatever lays waiting below had fought hard to reach beyond its prison. These fragile roots had been the beginning of what now dominates the entire valley of the island. The reason they swayed lay beneath the earth.

My legs ache. The darkness is only broken by bioluminescent fungi that dot the cave walls. Sickly greens and aquiline blues. I nearly trip when the stairs meet solid ground, and I hold on to the cold wall for support. Water trickles down it, and there's a small hole that scatters light onto a strange scene.

Not because it is, indeed, strange. Rather, it is painfully ordinary. Human.

An abandoned mining site.

Rusted picks lay in a discarded pile, some of the handles having rotted away. Hammers and chisels dot the ground. Decay twitches my nostrils. This place is ancient, carved hundreds of years ago, at least. There are no jackhammers or industrial rock breakers in sight.

The roots coalesce upon one wall. It's bricked over, excess bricks and mortar abandoned at the foot of it. The plant matter undulates and swells at my presence, an unfamiliar scent overwhelming that of decay.

I find a pick with an intact handle. It's heavy. I wish I'd eaten some of that trapped deer, but I have no idea how to carve up an animal for meat. No tools for it, either. Not sure I have the stomach for it.

My hopes, as fragile as they are, lay behind this wall.

I bring the end of the pick down against the bricks. I can't avoid the roots, and I feel their pain. A buzzing fills my mind, prickles my nerves, but whenever I stop, the air grows dense with impatience.

There are no words, but I know. It's instinctual, and I push through my exhaustion.

In the forest, I've seen no signs of humanity. It's wild and natural, untouched by industry or extraction. This is the first spot I've seen since the lodge where I've felt the presence of man.

And this place is so much older than the modern lodge, with its panoramic windows and automation.

Long ago, many years—perhaps centuries—before the hunting lodge was created, humans had ventured far into the north to seal this place shut.

To lock whatever is behind it inside.

A prison with no guards, abandoned to time.

Now I batter away at their ancient work. Mortar and brick chip away, bit by bit.

I've never given in to the instinct towards nihilism. Even as the climate got hotter, wars became more brutal, and slavery made a comeback, I held on to hope.

By the time nukes were dropped on civilians, opposition to war had been almost entirely snuffed out. The city-states all had their own shit to deal with. Their own civilians gave way to barbarism, and dealing with the war-machine was political suicide.

They gave up trying to resist, but I can't turn off this part of me that cares. Not just about those I know and love, but all of humanity. For all its flaws and faults, I've always felt a connection, the intricate web of life.

Whenever bitterness or hate edges in, resentment for the loneliness in my own life, I remember it does not have to be this way. This is not preordained. Humans are not hard wired for violence.

Whenever despair threatens me, I think of Aimi. Of the simple, beautiful, miraculous life she had before it was stolen away.

A better world is possible, and I have always tried to play a minor role in contributing to that hopeful dawn.

Now I'm trying to unleash something that's been locked away for reasons I don't understand.

I can almost picture the signs posted around this place, like that long-term nuclear waste warning.

This place is not a place of honour... no highly esteemed deed is commemorated here... nothing valued is here.

What is here was dangerous and repulsive to us. This message is a warning about danger.

The danger is in a particular location... it increases towards a centre... the centre of danger is here... of a particular size and shape, and below us.

The danger is still present, in your time, as it was in ours.

And still, I pick away at the stone.

I dig towards the centre of danger.

This place has been abandoned for so long, their tools left behind. Why?

As I bash through layers of old mortar, made weak by the cracks that had been exploited by the roots, I find strange markings. Occult symbols etched into the stone? Or maybe they are warning symbols of some culture, not my own. Something before the big wars and the destruction of the satellite networks fractured humanity.

"Ah!"

The pick hits air on the other side, and I stumble forward.

Sweat drips down my middle, along my torso. My black hair is matted to my forehead. My thin shirt clings to my skin.

I'm almost there.

The strange, kindred spirit is so close.

I haphazardly bash through more of the stone and mortar until I have a hole big enough to get through. My eyes are wild, manic, but everything is so dark. I can't see a damn thing.

At least, not at first.

Not until the roots begin to glow with that eerie bioluminescent light. Purple, red. Different from the fungi. They look like veins, and they glow brighter as I descend into the unknowable darkness.

CHAPTER 9

The floor is polished rock, obsidian like the rocks above, reminiscent of black glass. As if something ancient had struck here and turned everything into a sheet of that sheer stone.

The roots pulse ever so softly, like veins, the artery pulsing away from its heart; a door.

It's massive, metal. A padlock dangles from a mighty eye latch, living roots having penetrated it until steel gave way to plant matter.

There's no handle. This door is not made to be opened. I pry at a divot, but my bare hands can't budge it. The door is too old, too heavy, too rusted.

I fall to my knees, trembling with exhaustion. My weak body aches, blood throbbing in my temples. The stone is preternaturally cold against my back, sweat drenching the back of my shirt. I sob, but I'm too dehydrated to cry.

The roots glow brighter, red, pulsing to the rhythm of my heart.

"I need a second," I whine. The entity disagrees, impatience growing thick in the tepid, underground air. My legs tremble as I force myself up, lifting the pick once more.

I have nothing to lose.

My life was forfeit the second I woke up in this place.

Forfeit the second I trusted Leet.

Now I'm trusting something that wore his face in my dreams.

Fitting.

I bring the pick down to the divot with newfound precision.

I've gone insane. This isn't at all like how I felt after Aimi's death. That was all inept rage, lashed out in every direction. The injustice of it, the horror of her death, was bad enough. But the collective resignation and acceptance of such atrocities broke me. The news ran that mass murderer's face. Let him read his PR statements over and over again until it seeped into the collective consciousness of NV.

It was no longer just his word. As far as they were concerned, it was the truth, and no evidence to the contrary would convince them otherwise.

I was never insane. I was gaslit into believing that giving a shit about other people, about the world, was wrong.

This time is different.

This time I'm literally following my dreams, trusting in sentient grasses and moss.

Maybe this is all an elaborate hallucination, brought on by all those berries I ate. Sometimes people see fucked up shit when they're tripping, and they're convinced those visions are real. Am I trapped in a cave? Or am I held captive back at the lodge, just concocting this fucked up story of survival as a coping mechanism.

I try to use the pick as a lever, but it doesn't budge. All my time out here in the middle of nowhere has weakened me. Too much running and climbing and swimming. Too little food. Cortisol has flooded my nervous system, coiling around my muscles, tightening them.

I slump to my knees after another attempt, my chest heaving as I breathe in. It's hard work and so far, nothing. Not an inch. Not a centimetre of movement.

Tears spring to my eyes, a weak trickle that relieves none of my tension.

I heave a quiet sob.

For my plight.

For my insanity.

What am I doing?

It can't be real.

My back presses into the wall. The roots match my pulse, warmth flowing through them. It's comforting, and I lose track of time as I cry in self pity.

Something tickles my ear, and I instinctively try to bat it away. It finds my ear cannel, and one of those delicate roots penetrates my body with precise intention. Sentience.

A flash of memory flickers to life in front of me.

It's not my memory.

The colours are strange, objects emitting waves of energy.

A chisel. A hammer. Careful, refined tools. My gaze drifts to the corner of the chamber, hidden still in darkness. I see them, and yet I don't, because it's pitch black.

The root retreats from my ear, glancing along the outer shell as it joins its colony along the wall.

Did it give me the insight?

I'm losing it.

Only one way to prove that.

"I didn't check that corner before. So, if there's a hammer and chisel there, then..."

Then what, Shayde?

Then something else knew they were there, and that something else showed me they were there. Something that talks to me without words. Something that is connected to this elaborate root system.

Fear grips me as I stand on fawnish legs.

Fear of being wrong.

Fear of being right.

I grope in the darkness and find nothing. Nothing at all. The vision was just a delusion. My mind losing all grip on reality. I am damned, having fled to this hopeless place, doomed to starve to death while hiding from—

I feel it. First one handle. Then another.

I take the objects into the dim light of the roots' glow. A hammer and chisel. Old, but sturdy. A very fine set of tools despite their age.

Just as—what—the fucking *root* told me they would be?

Curiosity gets the better of me.

If death waits for me beyond that door, then at least it is a death of my own choosing. Few have a say on how they go out. Fewer still who wake up on this nested island.

I've never used a hammer and chisel before, but I

understand the basic premise. When I return to that divot, I place the chisel inside, then tap the hammer on the hilt.

Nothing much changes at first, and I experiment with it. A clump of rust chips away. Then another. Hours drag on as the pile of rusted metal grows at my feet.

I chip away more and more until the seams where the door meets the frame are clean.

How long has it been since I was on the surface? My stomach hasn't growled in protest, and even the ache of my muscles has dimmed. I've pushed my body past what I've thought possible, and still, I continue on.

I widen the divot, black stone and metal joining with the rust.

When finally it's wide enough to use the pick, it feels lighter rather than heavier.

I laugh. Manic. It echoes around the room, bouncing off the smooth stone before being swallowed by the roots. They pulse with excitement, the red glow burning brighter. The door groans and gives a metallic scream as I wedge it wide enough for my emaciated form to squeeze through.

The glow is subtle in the outer chambers, but inside, it is intense. I shield my eyes against the full colour of it. Red bleeds into a strange emerald glow, almost sickly, wrong. My breath lodges in my throat as a pungent odour assaults me. It's saccharine, too sweet, too metallic. I choke on it.

A sane woman with choices, any choices, would not have done what I did.

I squeeze through the gaping door into what lay beyond.

CHAPTER 10

The inner chamber is circular. The walls are rimmed with metal bars.

Wasn't the bedrock enough?

They needed more to contain their prisoner?

Intertwined through it all are the familiar roots, though they are far bigger, pulsating. They glisten like oil, the greenish glow shimmering off their surfaces as I step in.

At the centre of it is a mass of strange, tumorous life. The source of the roots that had reached up and up, through multiple prison walls, to infect the plant life above.

Is this it then?

Great.

My saviour is a cluster of roots. Some invasive species, surviving when most other life on the planet have died off.

Disappointment consumes me.

Maybe it's the hunger or the exhaustion or the fact that I'm on the run from being hunted by my fellow man, but I'd been hoping for something amazing. I slump down, too tired to even cry, and I just stare at it.

Freeing it won't even do much. It already had found a way to escape its prison. Now it can more readily grow, choking out native life on this cursed island. It can swallow the land for all I care. Swallow everything, starting with me.

My vision blurs from hot, angry tears.

For once, I thought I was special. Important. Doing something that would make a difference, as fucked up as that all is. My dreams convinced me I mattered, and that if only I could free this thing, it would all be worthwhile.

For a couple of days, I had a purpose. A reason to live.

I should have known better than to let my defenses down, but those little roots had found my crevices with as much skill as it'd exploited any crack in this prison.

There's a sickening sound and I rub my eyes.

Spots of light dance in my vision, obfuscating the burgeoning sight before me.

The strange, egg-like pods in the cluster of roots begin to crack and break open.

My breath is stolen from my chest as I stare in awe as it awakens.

It is no plant.

No tree.

No root thing.

Whatever it is, it is beyond my understanding. Something belonging to a more primal epoch.

A long, dark limb, tipped with a clawed hand, emerges, glistening with a black slime. It's larger than a human's by double, encased in something hard rather than flesh. Another joins it, then another.

Four limbs hold its torso up as it rises from a long hibernation, a lispy trill echoing around the cavern.

Sharp cracks split the air as it breaks from its old root structure, its old shell, like a crustacean finishing a metamorphosis into something new. It discards the egg with a splatter and rises to its full size.

I cower as it towers over me, leaning back on its hind limbs. It is at least eight feet tall. I'm just over five feet. The wall is wet as I press into it, trying to disappear into the roots. As if they could conceal me, hide me from its progenitor.

Its neck stretches out, its head a long, flared helm that's more similar to a stag beetle than a mammal. Its massive arms reach out, and more goop drops to the floor, forming a luminous puddle. It's almost like radioactive waste.

My heart is in my mouth as its maw opens, glistening fangs a shiny silver in contrast to the rest of its dark mass that glints emerald in the light. I don't see eyes at first, until I realize the big, multi-faced gem-like protrusions must be that. Something almost reptilian, if not for its insectoid nature.

Two more limbs come unfurled at its side, smaller than the first set. Whereas the large ones bear massive clawed fingers, these ones end in shell-like protrusions that reminds me of a tortoise shell.

A great tail lashes through the air with a whip-*crack*, sundering what remains of its former cocoon. The thick shell explodes, and I duck to avoid the shrapnel.

What have I done?

What chthonic creature have I unleashed?

I stare, transfixed, as this thing awakens. It is more terrifying and awe-inspiring than anything I've ever imagined before. It's beyond dreams or nightmares, something that doesn't belong here, and yet is so beautiful in its horror.

My lips part, and maybe I scream, but I can't hear it or feel it. For a moment, I'm simply consumed as I stare at something no human should behold. I want to look away as my brain begins to melt, unable to comprehend the aberration that looms over me.

I break it down into its parts. Its spindly limbs. Two large arms. Two small arms. A triangular torso with wide shoulders that narrow as it reaches its abdomen. Two muscular legs that protrude at its side with more joints than a human.

The clawed fingers are the size of a large dagger. It could rend me apart with a flick of its wrist.

I think I'd have pissed myself if I hadn't sweated and cried out every ounce of fluid in me. I'm desecrated, a shell of myself, and I cower as it moves towards me. Its two big forearms hit the smooth stone on either side of me, pressing in closer.

The room is silent, but the energy is cacophonous. The root-rimmed walls throb with panic, disconnected from the creature that controlled it.

Its head is a couple of inches from mine.

There's a strange sound, like water pouring over rocks. It's inhaling my scent.

Its tongue is terrifying as it extends out of its maw. Black and thick, with backswept spikes along its outer edges on both sides. It tastes my scent on the air as a lizard would do. The pointed, teeth-like protrusions slide back, inert.

When the muscle pushes against my throat, I'm catatonic.

It tastes my skin. My sweat.

I don't shrink away. The warmth is comforting. It's the first moment of waking comfort I've had, the first contact with a living thing I've experienced in weeks.

Touch-starved.

Betrayed by the only person I trusted.

I let the phantasm lick my throat, its tongue thicker than my neck. It's learning me. Probing me. It doesn't speak, and I can't find words. My fear is too great to access that part of my brain.

The slithering muscle trails down my neck to my arms, then up to my face. It's wet and yet dry, like a cat's tongue, covered in tiny barbs that don't hurt but are tactile.

Its two smaller arms reach out. Its tortoiseshell palms crack open, and six glistening appendages emerge. They're silvery like its teeth, but supple. One hand grasps my waist, as the other holds my skull.

I don't move, fear wrapped around me as I stare at its arthropod eyes. Two of its silvery digits sink into my ears, penetrating my ear canal just as the root had before. I squirm, trembling with disgust, until the world melts away.

I was wrong.

There's no monster in front of me. At least, not of the inhuman variety.

It's Leet. His hand on my head, as if he'd just been caressing my face, brushing back my hair. Handsome, smiling Leet, looking at me with endless pride and affection. His black eyes twinkle, his dimple pronounced.

"You did it."

Tears are hot in the corner of my eyes and they begin to fall, warmth flooding me.

"I did," I reply, and I'm shocked I did it. That I could do it. "I knew I'd find you here. That you wouldn't betray me. You'd never make a deal with the Umbridge family. Not after all they've done. Not after Aimi."

It's not Leet.

Some part of me knows that.

It's a delusion, warping my mind, my memory, but I'm slipping between the veil of two realities to make one that I can stomach. One where Leet is the man I needed him to be.

I know I'm being a fool.

I loved, and I was played. Giving into this fantasy will not change reality, but Leet's gaze is soft as he caresses my cheek, and I want to believe. I've trusted something horrible out of desperation, but it's offering me a reprieve from its creche, and I'm eager to take it.

"We are kindred spirits, Shayde."

I don't hear his voice with my ears, but with my mind. Our communication bypasses the need for language, a direct line of knowledge shared through an alien linking of minds. It can only communicate with me when in physical contact. When part of it is inside of me. The berries were part of it.

"I felt your rage and hatred from across space. Through the many millions of little follicles I extended to the surface," it says.

It.

They.

He.

It's hard to call it 'it' when it is looking like Leet, talking in the voice of a civilized man. I'm uncertain if it has a gender. It doesn't seem to know, either. I don't sense a preference between any of the terms.

"Your need for vengeance spoke to mine. Even now, as a long hunger gnaws at me." Leet grins, a glint in his eyes. Menace dwells in both.

A sane woman would run screaming from it, or at least try. Flee to the surface, take my chances with the humans.

Instead, I don't budge as he leans in and kisses my lips.

His tongue enters my mouth, and I caress it with my own. For a moment, it's sweet and passionate. Tender.

The illusion is shattered at the visceral sensation of a monster's barbed tongue sliding past my tonsils, filling my throat. I gag, my airway blocked off, but the muscle is too thick to resist. At any point, those protrusions along the side could flare out and rip me open from the inside out.

I buck upwards, and Leet's hand wraps around my waist, holding me in place. His tongue flicks, swells, and I can't breathe. It's going to suffocate me! The muscle pulls back, then dips down my throat again, tasting my insides, penetrating my throat. I spasm and buck, but I can't resist it. The world goes hazy until it finally slithers back out. My neck feels swollen, and I cough, sputtering for air.

I'm playing a dangerous game.

No, that's ridiculous.

I'm not playing a game at all.

I've freed something horrific, and I'm not in control at all.

For the first time in my life, the thought doesn't upset me. I brush my thumb along Leet's jawline as I swallow back oxygen.

Worlds blur together. I know it's not him, and I know

he can't give me what I've always wanted from Leet. But I also feel the same connection he speaks of, something primal and dark and terrifying. I've always tried to suppress those feelings, but this being controls them, holds onto them like a precious jewel, and makes me feel less afraid.

"What are you?"

Not-Leet's head tilts, his dark eyes gleaming. Silence reigns between us for a moment before he smiles again.

"Let me show you," he says as he caresses my side with one hand.

Suddenly, the chamber melts away. I am catapulted through time and space into a memory that should never be mine.

Centuries pass in reverse in the blink of an eye. Long, tedious centuries. Until finally it comes to a time when it wasn't alone. When it was a small thing, the size of a boy; almost the shape of a boy. It looked more human then than it does now. But still, it wasn't human.

The garb of the men is antique. Centuries out of date. Europeans who came with the young thing, back when this island was not an island but land, frozen year round in ice and snow. History class had called it permafrost.

They were friends. Companions. When they'd invited it on an expedition, it was happy to join them.

It trusted them.

They sealed it away.

It screamed in its awful, alien tongue for someone who wasn't there.

Who didn't care.

Who had betrayed them.

The bubbling, shrill sound echoed in a barren chamber.

There are no roots. Just metal and stone and freezing cold air, colder than I've ever felt before.

Then I'm back in time further. Upon the boat that had taken them into the far north. It chittered with excitement, watching the seas writhe with hundreds of thousands of fish. The water was alive with them, a mass of silvery bodies that jumped and swam beneath the surface.

Its tail whipped out, spearing one, and the captain clapped it on its back in approval.

Then back, back in Europe. An island. The naval colony of England, I think, before the wars.

Sea birds cry in the distance as the memory of a large manor flickers in my mind. It's beautiful, made of tanned brick, and I gape in awe. The skies are so clear, the blue so bright, I nearly drop to my knees. Grass and bushes and trees are vibrant dots of green and orange and red. There's a smell in the air that I have no words for, but the monster does. Autumn. It's crisp and clean and earthy in a way I've never experienced before.

Animals move in the distance, and beautiful little insects flit around the flowers. Bees. Butterflies. I've never heard of them before, but the creature knows them. A bird finds a worm and flies off, unconcerned with the aberrant child or the woman in the dark veil.

Was this what the world once was? Before the smog and the acid rain and the war and the nukes and the Great Boil Up that burned most of the equator? This was what humanity created and then destroyed?

I'm so distracted by the elysian visage of the Earth that once was that I have to force myself to look away. Tears blur my eyes.

The woman on the front porch of the manor is pale and plain, but lovely. Her eyes are the colour of the ocean, and he loved her then. She kisses him, caressing his face with the back of her black lace gloves.

The swell of powerful emotions are complicated in a familiar way. She betrayed him. That love had been twisted. She had sent it away, to be sealed in that prison on this recursive island for eons.

The woman—a mother?—had disposed of him. An ugly secret. Something she feared. She wanted rid of this boy who was not a human, but was not quite a monster.

At first, she'd tried to hide it in the deep dark caverns beneath her manor home. The caverns there, though big and dark and hidden, could not contain it. It kept getting free. A tiny creature roaming the English countryside.

It had eaten... things.

Animals.

Livestock.

Pets.

It did not know better. It needed to survive, and its instinctual urges were only natural. There was so much wildlife then, so many sources of food, but it was hungry, growing. Its chitinous shell was constrictive, and it needed energy.

It sobbed against its mother, as a human boy might, begging for forgiveness, for a crime it did not understand.

The memory changes, is no longer a memory. I feel as it grows big and tears into her, making sport of shredding her being until it is a mess of blood and gore.

This part did not happen. It was mere desire. Like the fantasies I've had of doing awful things to Leet.

I stand in the altered memory, seeing the giant hulk, splattered in blood, body heaving.

I smile.

He never told me what he is, but now I know. A kindred spirit.

"It's been so long, though. I'm certain she's ashes in the ground by this point. I can only hope she suffered for her betrayal."

The creature's spines click as they erect in fury at my words.

It stands up to its full height and lets loose a terrifying sound, like nothing I'd ever heard before. The vision of the foggy land distorts like ripples on the surface of a pond.

I cringe in horror for my misstep.

I've sent it into a frenzy, robbing it of its revenge rather than satiating it.

Fear freezes my blood in my veins, and I stare at it in terror, waiting for the end.

This is it.

I was so fucking foolish to think that I could trust anything ever again.

Kindred spirit!

I'm such a dumbass.

I wait for the strike, but it never comes. When my eyes open, it's back in its original form. Its true form. Its tendril remains in my ear, warm and ticklish and terrifying.

"We will see." I sense its smile, rather than see it. The hard shell of its face is frozen, expressionless, the alien features unable to convey the human emotions it feels.

It reaches out to caress my cheek.

"For now... your revenge will be mine. And it will sate

my hunger," it says, before leaning down to kiss my lips once more.

There's nothing natural about this. Its mouth is inhuman, its body even more so. Its anger is terrifying, but its affection is unsettling. Maybe it's just because of how my body responds, my blood thrumming with heat, my emaciated limbs trembling as it pushes in against me. They no longer look like Leet, and I'm under no illusions of what's happening.

Of how it's responding to me.

Of how I'm responding to it.

Chapter 11

I'm starving. I'm on an isolated island. My only companion betrayed me to a bunch of arms dealers. Did Leet know what they were going to do to me? Did he think they'd just slap me on the back of the hand?

At best, he knew I'd be sent to the prison colony for hard labour in the poisoned mines.

Likely I'd be tried for treason and drawn and quartered, dragged through the street by the coal spewing ATVs. I'd be made an example of.

The pain cuts deep. It was one thing for my parents to deny me, to punish me for a sense of justice they never shared. My girlfriend, well... It was a high school thing. I can't hold that against her too hard, despite how much I needed her.

I've been so lonely for so long. No one has ever understood me. I finally met someone who I thought got me, and I was so wrong. It almost cost me my life to miscalculate Leet's kinship with me.

But the connection I have with the chimera wearing the

illusion of him is deep. Intimate. Immediate. I don't just hear the honied lies that my fragile heart longs to hear. I feel them, as if they're my own emotions.

The ground goes soft beneath me as I swoon, but four hands support me. Explore me.

I crave its affection. Its touches and protection.

My head spins from my long, arduous time in the wilderness. Not-Leet pulls back. He is aware of my vulnerable state, the same as I am.

"You are weak..." it says, and the image of Leet fades. I am no longer in that bucolic eden, but in that pulsating chamber. A great sorrow overwhelms me, and I slump down further. I've had the slightest taste of Eden, and I want to lose myself in that memory, despite how upsetting it is to the monster.

It's selfish. I resist the impulse to share in more of its memories of the past.

"Rest..." it bids me before its slithering fingers slip out of my ears.

With its four arms, it lays me down on a spongy soft mass of... something awful, no doubt.

The giant creature fills the doorway. It's too large to fit, but with its multi-jointed body, it folds in upon itself until it is small enough to dart through.

I'm exhausted. My arms ache from all the mining for monsters, and the rest of my body is still suffering from my time as prey. I can't fight sleep any longer. Darkness claims me.

This time I don't dream. At least, not the shared dreams that it and I have been having. No, this time the dreams are all too human and expected. They are nightmares. Fears of what this thing could do to me. Would do to me. How much of a fool I was to free it.

I had seen glimpses of its past, saw it rending a horse apart with its claws when it was just a tiny creature. A horse. A full-sized horse! If it could do that to a horse, what chance did I stand?

My nightmares answer that question.

No chance at all.

The slice of its claws, the gnashing of its fangs as it crushed thick bones, snacking on them as a packet of crisp biscuits.

My sleeping mind reflects on the horror of our first face to face encounter. My unconscious state peels back the layers, raw flesh exposed to the wicked light of day. How disconnected from reality, from myself, I had been to take it without screaming and pissing myself.

If that moment had come before I was starving, delirious, and still holding residual hallucinogenic berries in my veins, I would have done that and more.

It is not a creature meant for our world.

It did not belong.

Even if it felt some kinship with me due to our shared bitterness, rage and anger, how long can that last?

How long before I do something that triggers a bestial rage like what I saw in its rush of memories?

So many memories it had implanted in me in so little time.

It's only in dreams that I can process the deluge of memories. The miners laid their trap, drawing it into this cell. They closed the door. It knew, then, that it had been misled, and it lured a man close.

The man's arm was ripped from his torso as easy as one might tear a chicken leg off a well-cooked bird.

That had been its last proper meal in centuries. I can almost taste the blood, the flesh, as the bones crack in its powerful maw. I wake screaming.

The scent of blood and meat follows me into the waking realm.

Raw, gamey meat and coppery blood.

The monster is hunched over a carcass of a deer. The one from earlier. It bleeds out as claws slice through its thick hide as if they were the sharpest knives on earth.

Whether I faint or fall back asleep, I'm not sure.

I traipse through more of its memories, disjointed, non-linear. There is an aching loneliness, a familiar sense of otherness that follows it. In all its time on the surface, it has never known another of its kind. It does not know if it is the only one of its kind.

The first time it consumed raw flesh was a powerful experience. It didn't know, then, that it was doing something wrong. There was a base pleasure in giving in to its instincts, the rush of the hunt, the reward of a filling meal. A cow, it learned later. Owned by one of the woman's neighbours. She had to pay for it, and she scolded it. Taught it shame for doing what came naturally.

The meat is tender. Pure. Even though it's raw, I taste it as the monster had, and I relish how satiating that bloody meat is. Dreams and reality clash, my teeth tearing into spongy flesh.

It's not raw, but it's not cooked, either. I gag, pulling away at first out of some cultural repulsion at the idea of uncooked meat, even as I risk starving. The creature reaches out and its digit slides into my ear again.

It hurts, the tendril too large for my ear canal, but the sensation fades as its voice echoes in my mind.

"I prepared it. It's safe for human consumption."

The phantasm of Leet reappears. Obsidian exoskeleton replaced by pale flesh, insectoid eyes narrowing into human ones. A carved mouth with hard protrusions softens into a smile.

He presses the deer meat back to my lips.

I'm too weak to resist, and its reassurance batters down the last of my revulsion. I open my mouth and, for the first time in weeks, I taste something hearty. Meat is scarce in NV. Over the years, I've only had a few pieces for important celebrations.

When I got into Owasis Prep, my parents took me to a restaurant that cost a month's rent. We ordered the cheapest cut of Prat, a genetic hybrid between a pig and a rat. It was so rich it melted in my mouth.

That was one of the last happy memories I have with my parents, and waves of warmth flood from the creature as I reminisce. I moan, then flush in embarrassment.

My walls are coming down, my guarded self becoming vulnerable in my needy state, and I don't like it. But I don't have the luxury of pride, so I continue to chew and then wait for more; a toddler being finger fed.

My stomach churns. It's been so long since I've eaten more than a few handfuls of berries. The rare deer meat is a shock to my system, and pulses of gentle comfort flow from it to me. It soothes my guts enough to digest the food.

"Good girl," says Not-Leet as it feeds me like I am an

injured animal it is nursing back to health. Though we are very different species, our psychic link grows stronger, and with it, understanding.

I am the first human it has communicated with. Before it was locked away, it did not know it could communicate. It was only once it was forced to survive as an elaborate series of roots and berries that it learned.

"Eat up. Get strong," it tells me with a care to its voice the monster could never convey in its true form.

Though there are hundreds of pounds of meat, an unthinkable bounty, I cannot tolerate much of it at once. My stomach has shrunken away, and it pains as I force it to expand.

Safety and satiation lull me back to sleep. As I drift off, I see memories, not my own. How it prepared the meat. How it had used acid to 'cook' it, rather than heat. The thought of where the acid came from jolts me awake with a cough, as I struggle not to vomit.

Time has passed. I'm not sure how much. The deer has been moved, preserved in a cold section of the arcane cell. It still hovers over me, a child nursing a wounded bird. A canteen of water is in one of its clawed hands.

It's spattered with blood.

I can only assume it once belonged to the man I had bludgeoned to death. How long has it been? It feels like only moments, my weariness still present.

The water is cold, fresh. There is no grit in it. It doesn't tingle my mouth with chemicals.

I drift back to sleep to the sounds of it returning to its own meal.

Raw flesh.

Bone.

Strips of camo.

I walk through countless worlds in dream as my sleep draws on, until finally, it comes to me in another shared dream.

This one is more vivid than any of the others.

A neon city, way up high. Neo-Vancouver. It's a rare, clear day, and even as high as we are, I can see for miles around. The grey ocean, the floating island of garbage off the shore. There's a familiar buzz of electricity and construction and people, but the noise of the world drifts away into the distance.

It's so peaceful.

Surrounded by people, yet alone.

Except for Leet.

The new Leet that exists in my shared consciousness with a monster.

I smile.

There's a meal in front of us, eaten, and he's cleared away the dishes to the side. The candle between us has burned down to almost a stub, and there's some soft music in the background. The breeze on the balcony tussles my dark curls, and I laugh, brushing them out of my face. When Leet smiles in return, his dark eyes crinkle at the corner. It's genuine.

I can't remember ever seeing him so relaxed and content, and somehow I know that everything's fine.

It's a strange feeling, one I can't recall having before. Ever since I was a kid, I'd always felt that something was off. My parents called me a highly sensitive child, sometimes affectionately, often dismissively. I'd tell them of this injustice, or that catastrophe, and they'd tell me to stop looking for things to be upset about, but I didn't know how to close my eyes to it all.

In this dream, though, there's nothing to be mad about. The world is at peace, and life is thriving in the neon city that sprawls out around us.

Leet touches my face, guiding my curls behind my ear.

"I love when you let your hair down."

"The wind is making me regret it," I laugh, and then the wind stills in response.

Leet grins at my words, his dark eyes sparkling as he takes me in, as if I'm the most gorgeous work of art he's ever seen.

He's enthralled with me.

"It gives you a wild look. Like you're a force of nature, sent unto earth to rectify mortal wrongs," he tells me in a reverential voice. It's not just a line. He feels the truth of his own words as sincerely as I do the truth that the world usually sucks.

"Wouldn't that be nice," I say, unable to hide how much I wish that were true. A calling that's always resonated with me. "With you, maybe that's possible, though."

Leet looks so good. He always looks good, but this night he looks especially so. In his fancy, tailored suit, perfect for his tall, lanky frame, he looks out of time and place, and yet, I'm enticed.

He reaches out to me, his hands so big, his fingers so long, to caress along my cheek, back to my ear and into my hair.

"Anything is possible when we work together. Your

heart and mind to guide my strength and skills..." he says as he cradles my face and leans forward. Our knees touch as we sit at that table overlooking the city. He hovers near, almost kissing me, but he instead touches his forehead to mine, the tip of his nose to mine. "We are fated for one another, Shayde..."

I've longed to hear those words, to matter so much to someone. All my life. Decades of just wanting to be special to someone. Important.

And with him, it's not just words. It's beyond language. It's an understanding, a shared consciousness, a belief that I feel as well. He's right. This impossible meeting must be a part of something larger than ourselves. We can change the world. I can guide him, teach him all the things his mother neglected to.

I'm the one that closes the distance, my lips finding his, brief and soft at first before becoming more passionate.

Everything he knows of the modern world comes from me, plucked from my mind, and so too does his skill with kissing. He's the ideal kisser for me, his tongue against mine. Our psychic link instructs him, and he takes the lead. His tongue massages mine, retreating when it becomes too much. This time he doesn't choke me on it, instead becoming more restrained.

It's so satisfying to melt into his embrace and let it follow such a perfect, natural course.

We make out for hours, it seems. His big hands caress my body, combing through my hair. He's so tender and caring, even as he grows more assertive, guiding things along. It's hard to put this magical scene alongside the reality.

And so, I don't.

"I want you," he says, our lips puffy from all the kissing, his voice raw and rough.

In reality, in the real world, we're in a dank cave surrounded by pulsating organic matter. He's something otherworldly, almost insectoid more than mammalian. Instead of warm flesh, he has a cold, unfeeling exoskeleton.

I'm not even sure if he has a penis or a vulva or a cloaca or something different.

Even knowing that doesn't diminish the truth. My body aches for more.

It's fucked up, but I don't care. This time in the wildness has changed something fundamental about me. Maybe it's his influence, his consciousness weaving its way into mine, manipulating me.

That would make this a little easier. Recuse me of responsibility. There's freedom in pretending that I'm just a hapless puppet, dancing to his design.

It's not true, though. While we have a psychic link, I am still my own person. My consciousness, and my desires, are my own.

"I want you too."

CHAPTER 12

He lifts me with incredible ease. He's stronger than the real Leet, who, though he could've lifted me too, would've at least given a grunt. But no, my version of him is powerful beyond anything the original Leet could aspire to.

He carries me inside to the posh penthouse. Leet's apartment, bought with blood money. A massive bed is encased in expensive silk sheets. They're cool and slippery under my naked spine.

"You're so very special, Shayde... so very, very special. In a way I didn't think any person could be."

I help undress him, pale and unblemished skin unveiled beneath his suit. His lean torso and broad shoulders are almost as I remember them, though different. The intricate tattoos have warped into something else that doesn't have the same connection to his past. His limbs are longer, the skin nearly translucent over his muscles.

There are just enough subtle changes to dull the anger I have towards this body, the thing wearing Leet's form. He's become someone new, someone without the baggage of reality. An amalgamation, a fantasy.

He unfastens the buckles of my tech-wear pants. I pull off my tight black top. My breasts are bared before him, and I flush, glancing away. My ribs are no longer visible, my hips soft and less angular. I've never had the supple curves of a wealthy woman, and I envied the rolling hills and delicate valleys of their figures.

We always struggled to eat well enough, growing up. Especially after I was kicked out. Maybe that's why this stint of starvation isn't as devastating to me.

I've always been self-conscious about my body. What could a monster think of it? How would he even find anything in my appearance appealing? We are alien to each other, despite the skin he wears in my dream.

He leans over me, cupping one breast in his big hand. It's too large, disproportionate to Leet's body. It encompasses one breast as his mouth circles over the other. His plush lips are soft and warm as his rapacious tongue circles my pink areola.

There's an inhuman quality to it, a roughness that is not unpleasant.

This is nothing like my one time with the real Leet. He is attentive, caring, and taking his time with me. Reverence guides every motion. His tongue—long still, though nowhere near as much as his real-life form—slides around my teat.

"You are beautiful... perfectly beautiful. I never imagined someone like you could exist," he says in a deep, husky voice.

A kittenish mewl escapes me, heat rising to the surface

of my skin. This is all in my mind, I know, but also... it isn't. It's taking place between the veil of reality and dream, and our physical forms aren't compatible.

The monster wearing a human body responds to my prurient interest.

If he's too gentle, he increases the pressure. Too fast, and he slows down to the perfect tempo. It's like becoming intimate with my own fantasies. With our psychic bond, I don't need to say a word for him to just *know* what I want.

It doesn't surprise me when he suckles my breast, despite that being a fantasy I could *never* share with anyone. Him fulfilling my secret cravings without my uttering a word; I sink deeper into the moment, yielding myself to him utterly.

He is gorgeous in my dreams. The man of my dreams. The man I had crushed on for so long, only better. More perfect. Made for me.

His hand massages one breast as he latches on the other. Contentment floods me, a flush of heat warming me all over. My shoulders relax, and I breathe at a calm, regular pace. There's no rush, and his enjoyment of tasting me radiates out of him.

My mouth parts in a moan. An alien vibration teases my nipple, which aches as it stiffens. My hips buck upwards, finding his thigh. I'm wet as I grind against that thick leg. He presses it further between me, encouraging my dry humping. My panties are soaked, but he's still not done tasting my chest.

He switches to the other tit, and there's a strange sensation of roughness, of a dull blade tracing the sensitive edge of my nipple. I gasp, remembering the serrated tongue. It toes the line between fact and fantasy.

Is this real?

Is that the creatures's tongue wrapping around my nipple, the long muscle hugging and tugging upon my sensitive bud?

A powerful flush of heat fills my body from my toes up to the top of my skull, and I lose control over my limbs. As the monster greedily sups from my breast, I submit to orgasmic pleasure. He guides me over that peak, an encouraging purr vibrating around my nipple as he latches on.

It's only once my orgasm has abated that one of his hands slides down, and he peels my sticky panties down my milky thighs. Every motion is one of reverence and desire. The butterfly kisses down my stomach are a reprieve from the intense sensations on my breasts, and I gather my breath.

I lose it once more as his tongue and lips find my pussy. Beginning slowly, he peppers my mound with affectionate kisses.

My orgasm fades as his long, agile tongue cleans me of my juices.

The sensation is unlike anything a partner has blessed me with before. His tongue is too thick, too rough, but he controls it. Always pressed up against my limits. I writhe and stare down at his hungry mouth as he devours me.

Flickers of reality intrude.

He is too wrapped up in the moment to maintain the perfect illusion. Between my legs is not Leet, but a giant, obsidian form.

Two large, clawed hands part my thighs, my flesh dimpled around the digits. The two smaller hands roam my flesh. I stare in horror as I watch that serrated tongue slip between my inner labia. Its tomia is relaxed along the muscle, for now.

He penetrates me with his long tongue, his nictitating membrane flicking over his eyes. It is thicker than anything that had been inside me before, and more agile. When the tip flicks against my cervix, I gasp in shock.

The ridged edges of his tongue become firm, though not dangerous. The sensation is unbelievable, and as I stare at the monster between my legs, it mutates. Leet is there, but my mind can't reconcile the feeling of his tongue with the human illusion. An eldritch mouth emerges from Leet's pale skin suit, just as a werewolf would peel back its human husk.

Their tongue retreats, then fills me again. Its tongue is too large to fit within me in a straight line, so it coils within me like a snake. My entire vagina is filled, bulging and stretching to unnatural angles. It licks against my inner walls, a hungry carnivore tasting me. He could devour me like this, starting with my sex.

Its fangs press against my outer labia, parting them open as he hungrily eats me out.

As the tip of its tongue teases against my cervix, the pain and pleasure are blinding. He has such control over his body in ways a human doesn't, and the tip shrinks until it's thin enough to taste me even there.

Even seeing the twisted shell of Leet, cracked open at the mouth to reveal the monster beneath, another orgasm claims me.

He laves every ounce of my juices, cleaning me up with reverential attention. When finally I can tolerate no more, his tongue retreats, my public mound shrinking as I'm emptied.

He rises, his broad shoulders on display. He slides a hand down his torso sensually until he's grasping at the base of that hard cock. It's bigger than Leet's, and Leet was not small by any measure.

I can't help but wonder.

What is this creature really holding?

Does he have human genitals?

I stop fighting so hard to keep reality at bay. There's something so obscene about it, because I know there's no stopping this. I don't want to stop it.

But when I see it, when I truly see it, I'm aware of how far gone I am.

The reality seizes me. The green, glowing cavern illuminates the ominous eight-foot monster looming over me. Its spear-like tail sways behind it, wagging like an excited puppy.

Dagger and sword like claws wrap around my sides, its strange slithering digits of one hand on my stomach and waist. The other reaches for a point between its legs, as its carbonous, almost metallic shell cracks open.

From that protective casing, a length of delicate flesh emerges, similar to the soft tendrils on its smaller hands.

Its phallus resembles a stinger. Long. Silver. Pointed at the tip. At first, it is only a few inches, but it lengthens, articulating in a serpentine manner as it extends towards my slit.

Its jaw doesn't move as I hear that delectable voice in my head.

"Don't ruin it by looking too close, my love..."

He releases the member as it moves under its own power. The gap closes between us, and its pointed tip runs along the length of my slit. It is supple, not as sharp as it looks, but I still tremble. I had thought its tongue was long and dangerous, but this is so much more phenomenal.

His hand with the soft tendril caresses my cheek. His prehensile cock nudges against my vulva. It's too terrifying, this reality. I obey, falling back into the fantasy, weaving between the two worlds with greater ease than before. My control is growing over it, and I push my fingers through Not-Leet's dark hair, kissing him affectionately. Passionately.

Knowing all the while that this very well could be my end.

It's a death far preferable to one at the hands of my own kind, though.

My monstrous lover gasps as his alien phallus presses in, beginning with the hook-like tip. It is narrow at first, and then grows thicker, and he has to put more force into it. I gasp as my slender pelvis is invaded, having to suck in breath as he gets to the thickest part of the stinger tip.

There is a brief reprieve as it is lodged within me. He trembles with pleasure as our parts lock together. He tests the seal, pulling back slightly, and is contented that he is knotted within me.

Lascivious desire courses through him as I wrap my arms up around his neck and kiss him again. There is no going back. He's rutting me like an animal, and I'm helpless to retreat. I fall deeper into the dream, stare up at Leet's loving eyes.

He presses in further between my legs, and his motions are slow, cautious. I am making love, and being made love to. I am not merely being *fucked*.

"You are so tight, Shayde. It is pleasurable to be within you like this. To love you like this. I am coming to understand it now. You are perfect."

His hips roll, his human cock pistons into me.

I can't help myself. My curiosity gets the better of me. Truth bleeds in at the edges.

He is not thrusting his hips. Instead, his hindquarters are locked in place as his thick, silver organ swells. There is something flowing through it, causing it to bulge and then shrink in a rhythmic pace. The soft flesh swells at the apex of my thighs before pumping thick fluids into my body.

The connection is stronger.

My ecstasy is shared with his, rising in time with his pleasure of my body.

The pure, undiluted sensation of bliss floods me. My head lolls back, my eyes flutter closed. A smile forms on my face as I pant for breath. I'm not just letting this monster take me. I want him to. The twin feelings of reality and fantasy blur, and my hips roll towards him until I find the right position.

He knows it, and he knows what to do. How to thrust, what angle, what tempo. It's almost as if I'm the puppet-master, and he's my obedient puppet, reacting and moving as I will it.

His clawed hands grip me tighter at my waist and hips. Both smaller hands go to my breasts, the soft tendrils plucking at my sensitive nipples. They form suction around them, my areolas becoming puffy with the pressure.

The tip of his stinger teases towards my cervix, but whatever it is flowing from his cock makes the sensation pleasurable rather than painful. A numbing agent, perhaps. He can hit me in my depths, make it hurt, but just that right amount. The way no person ever could without knowing my inner thoughts and sensations as well as I do.

"I want this," I hear his hissing voice in my head as he takes me. His pleasure—as strange and otherworldly as it is —is genuine. His desire for me may be performative, done in a manner that I can recognize and appreciate, but it's real. Our anatomies are compatible enough.

Maybe there is some humanity in them, or maybe it's the empathetic connection. I heard that most animals don't have sex for pleasure, but this monster is capable. I feel it almost as strongly as I feel my own orgasm budding in me. My limbs tremble, and I cling to him with growing urgency.

"Close!"

Its strange, rubbery finger-like appendages extend engulf more of my breasts until both are being suctioned by them. It keeps up that pace, its organ swelling and pumping with predictable regularity. Its hideous jaw falls open, fangs glistening as it rasps.

"Come for me." The alien voice reverberates in my brain, an undeniable order that could pass as instinct.

This thing, this monster, cares more for my pleasure than any human had. Its long, barbed tongue licks at my neck, up over my face. I part my lips to scream, and its tongue steals it away. I gag on it as it presses past my tonsils.

It hesitates long enough for me to take a swallow of air before it penetrates my throat once again.

My orgasm crushes me under its weight.

It's unlike anything I've experienced before, this other-worldly beast doing things to my body and brain that are unfathomable. I buckle and spasm, holding onto flesh that alternates to a hard exoskeleton and back again. My emaciated body has been tortured, but every ounce of bliss is found on its appendages.

Its strange, weapon-like member fills me like no man ever could.

I feel complete. Whole.

He arcs back his neck and lets loose a roar that crackles with static.

A torrent of... is it seed? I have no idea. But whatever he's filling me with is copious. The tip of his stinger pierces my cervix, flooding my depths. It makes me feel full in so little time until silvery fluid is dripping out through the tight seal of my loins upon him. It keeps flowing, coating the floor, splattering on my thighs as he empties his lust into me.

"Yes... Yes, my sweet," he rasps in my mind.

It's the best sex of my life, and while there's not a lot of competition, it's still a pretty damning indictment about the guy I once thought was the love of my life.

I'm sobbing as my orgasm ebbs, hot tears rolling down my cheeks as all that pent up anger and loneliness coalesce inside me. This monster has a way of finding the parts of me that hurt and soothing them in some primordial way that scares me as much as I grow hungry for it.

My arms wrap around his back, and he holds me as our

bodies return to normal. He can't withdraw his phallic organ, not right away. It remains within me, plugging his seed deep within me. His ribbed tongue retreats, licking away the tears I'd shed through my orgasm.

His body lacks the softness of a person's, but implanted atop me, holding me, I feel safe. Comforted. Pleasured. He is several feet taller than me, and his body encompasses mine. He draws me into his lap, his phallus still undulating, swelling and emptying into my depths.

"I will take out all the bad parts he left you with... and leave only those that please you, sweet Shayde," he says as much as asks. For he knows my answer already. The asking and saying is just a courtesy. A little nicety, so it doesn't seem he's assuming when in actuality he just knows.

Our minds dance together in ways no physical bodies could, and yet the formality of saying it gives it normalcy. In as much as what we have could ever be normal.

"What should I call you?"

He reached into the depths of my memories to find something special and suitable. A name from long ago, a special little title for a make-believe friend I had as a child. Something taken from stories I obsessed over in my youth, mixed and mangled into something new.

"Drelark," he says, his strange hand cupping my face. "Now relax... relax in my arms."

I soften, right as his carnal appendage rips from me with a suddenness that is only outdone by the shriek of pain inside me. The silvery flow of his fluids are marred by a trickle of ruby red blood.

I'm frozen, not even able to scream from the hurt as I

watch my body tremble and shake, as if no longer connected to me.

I begin to black out, but not before I see the most hideous sight. Drelark lowers down, and out of the bloody mess that came from between my legs, he eats some tiny, fleshy morsel.

Some part of me.

CHAPTER 13

I drift in and out of consciousness as I rest and recover. Each time I awaken, it is to the terrifying visage of Drelark, or the facade of his faux-Leet form, feeding me meat and berries.

The part he'd ripped from me had hurt, and it left me exhausted.

Time has lost meaning. I drift through it, my sleep a mix of terrifying nightmares and comforting dreams. The comforting dreams are Drelark, as he soothes the scars I'd tried so hard to ignore.

In those dreams, Leet takes me on journeys, missions of hope. We topple the corrupt, fascist government of NV. We expose war criminals. Military leaders, murderers of innocent men, women, children, taste justice.

Together, we travel to Kyoto, and I meet Aimi's neighbours. I smell the cherry blossoms, and they smell just like autumn. Drelark watches the moon rise over the ocean, the night so clear I can see the planets in the distance. He doesn't know the names, so we make them up. Cerulia. Ring-light. Rust.

Once, he shows me the sky dancing, vibrating with colours. Green, red, white. They wave like a flag, and though the memory is hazy, I cling to it. The sky is so beautiful, so expressive, and I hate that the smog has stolen so much from me. He wraps his arm around me, cooing. It's a raspy rattle, one that soothes some ancient part of my brain. My pain dulls, and I'm able to enjoy his memories of nature without the cruel pang of my longing that accompanies them.

The past was nirvana, and within my dreams, it returns. Nature reclaims the war machines, resilient plants cracking through the pavement and reaching towards the sun. The world is at peace, and it is thanks to us.

A fantasy, a utopian hope for the future. One that he and I helped usher in together, if only through my dreams. It's a vision of the world that has always been so out of reach on this corrupt plane of existence where justice is so elusive. When he gives me those snippets, it feels possible. Probable, even.

I'm reluctant to abandon that world, but he guides me back. At one point, he comes to me, not as Leet, but as Aimi. It's always been too painful for me to talk about my cousin, or the fact that I was witness to her last living moments. I had heard the tremor in her voice as she stared at death.

"I'm glad you were not there. You do not need to feel guilty that you did not die with me."

Her voice is just as I remember it, and I sob, even though this is all a lucid dream.

"Aimi," I whimper, and she embraces me. I'd only met her once in person, when I was a child, and she still smells like honeysuckle. The scent fills my lungs as I breathe her in. "It's so unfair."

"I know. I know. But no part of the blame lay with you."

"I should have done more! The government... I missed that protest, the one when I was sixteen. Maybe if I'd have been there, if more of us had shown up..."

"More would have died that day."

"No! No, if there were enough of us, they couldn't have killed us all. They would have had to listen to stop Umbridge's occupation of Japan!"

Drelark holds me, his gaze soft and sympathetic as he wears my memory of Aimi's body. It's less solid than Leet's, formed when I was still so young. Her kind eyes and full lips are the most consistent part of her.

Her garden grows and swells around us, undulating as the fronds of the island had.

"You were a child, but even then, you were thoughtful. It wasn't that you didn't attend the march because you didn't care, but that you'd only just gotten into Owasis Prep. You wanted a clean criminal record so that you could do something that really mattered. Infiltrate Umbridge, become a spy for the Western Resistance. Have you forgotten?"

I had.

As the protestors were gunned down, my patience ran out. I hacked my school, exposing the corruption of the administration. I was expelled. My parents disowned me. Nuclear explosions lit the very air on fire.

My time in the asylum cinched any plans I once had to become a spy. The records would always reveal that I was never a woman that could be a passive bystander of injustice.

"I forgot."

"Now you remember. You have never failed humanity, nor me. And there is still time for you to balance the scales."

Aimi's face fades into the distance, and as I wake upon the cold ground, I am filled with a warmth I've never experienced before. Contentment. Certainty. Some of the pain of my past has been soothed away, and even as I open my eyes to a dark, underground prison, I am not afraid.

Days have gone by since I freed him; no idea how many anymore.

The hunters promised my release after a week. Many have passed since then.

I'm alone, and the pain in my midsection is dissipated. This is a fever dream. Something brought on by stress and strange berries that have altered my mind. The trauma of my past seeking resolution before my death.

This is all a vivid hallucination.

There is no monster. I'm not in any pain. This is it, I've stayed long enough. I need to get home. Back to my life. Back to the work of exposing these fuckers for who they are, for what they do. It's time to follow the path that my younger self had wanted for me.

First thing first. Escape from these nested islands and the hunters looking for me. I don't trust they'll be true to their word, but a kernel of a plan is growing within me.

Since I woke in the Lodge, I've been running away from it when I should have been running towards it. If I could break into the Lodge and hack their systems, I could call a helicopter. Then I'd just have to figure out how to deal with the pilot, and get back to NV.

I'm almost at the door when an ominous figure descends from above. Drelark emerges from a slimy cocoon, brittle beneath the ooze. His gigantic form, obsidian as the darkest night, shimmers an other-worldly emerald in the fungal light.

Those long, terrifying fangs show before he drops to the ground, body curving around for a smooth landing.

He reaches for me, and I am not fast enough to avoid it, as his strange, non-clawed hand grasps my head, tendrils snaking into my mouth and ear. Suddenly I can hear him again, see him as this Leet-look-alike.

"Finally, you're awake," he says with such a disarming smile. As if he hadn't ripped a part of me out of my womb and ate it.

There's no hiding anything from him, not with him entering my mind. Everything is unfiltered, at least as far as I can tell, and he senses my confusion and horror before it even has words.

His smile falters. He caresses my cheek. While the illusion lasts, I don't feel the fact that his wriggling appendages are squirming inside my ear and mouth. I see the reality he wants me to see.

"You're upset..." he says with such a tone of seriousness and concern. "Oh..."

He plumbs my mind for the truth of it, seeing where my thoughts are lingering. "You didn't know?"

No, I don't know. I don't *want* to know. The things we did, that we had sex! It's all too much to wrap my fragile, human mind around, and expanding on any of those thoughts too far is like staring into the abyss. It's dangerous, and I have to look away.

His expression is genuinely sad as he holds my face.

"I removed a parasite, something he infected you with."

His arm wraps around my waist, and I don't resist as he pulls me into his comforting chest.

I tremble. The truth threatens me. Leet and I hadn't used protection, despite my telling him to use a condom. He laughed at me. Told me not to worry. I insisted. He ignored me. I wanted him so badly to like me. For him to reciprocate my feelings.

He'd impregnated me.

Drelark had...

My feelings are a hurricane, whipping around inside me, fuelled by rage. I'd thought the lack of my period was due to the starvation, not pregnancy! Yet even as I collapse, there's a part of me that recognizes the fear that had teased the edges of my mind ever since I arrived. I just hadn't been prepared to confront it.

Drelark pulls me in closer, that mellisonant chitter reverberating through my chest. I soften, my anxiety dripping away. It's something primal, somatic. The sound releases the tension from my muscles, putting me in a soporific state.

My anger dims, and since I never had time to think about what having a child could mean to me, I do not miss it. I do not feel violated, or robbed of agency.

Our connection is pure, undiluted through human language. I needn't ask if I can trust him, or believe him.

Our thoughts dance with one another's, spun together like a thread. Separate but intertwined.

"It was something that had to be done, so we can leave. And be together in the real world." His voice is as tender as his lips as he kisses my forehead.

In the real world with him. With this monster.

How fucked up is it that the first time I feel a genuine connection, and that someone wants the same things I do, on a cellular level, and it's this? Something from another world, feared and neglected and locked away for centuries.

In his own strange way, he's shown me more humanity than my own kin.

"Okay."

It's a simple word, not even a strong one, but it's heavy with meaning.

He squeezes me in his arms. His grip is powerful enough to crush me, but the pressure of it calms me.

With a big smile on his face, he pulls back.

"It's time for us to hunt, my love. It is time for your revenge."

His serrated tongue lashes out along its fanged maw, the reality bleeding through the illusion.

I smile, and for a moment, I imagine I, too, have razor sharp fangs.

The soulless men who got their kicks hunting a defenseless woman on an island are, for once, going to know fear.

CHAPTER 14

My breath is visible in the night air. It's so strange, and I watch the steam float from my lips, fascinated by the natural process. Frost prickles my lungs, my tank top leaving most of my flesh revealed so that it prickles with goosebumps.

I clutch myself, trying to adapt to my sometimes-intense shivering.

The wild north is extraordinary. It's hard to believe that this is part of the same planet as NV. Drelark's memories had given me insight into how much it's changed. When they arrived, it was covered in white, cold snow.

There were no trees back then, and it had been silent. The snow swallowed sound, and despite how flat the land was, it was a land made for stealth.

Sometimes the ice would groan, louder than thunder. Animals stalked for prey at dawn and dusk. The night sky was so clear at night, the stars and moon illuminating the world for miles around.

The expedition party had drilled into the ice, through

the permafrost. They were certain that down there, Drelark would be forever contained, but global warming and the Great Boil Up brought new life to this land. It softened the soil, released its clutches on its prisoner, and so Drelark, too, had evolved and grown.

His memories don't help me navigate the new landscape, and though the moon is bright, its light is intermittent through the clouds.

We travel at night, and we part the eye, travel through the valley. The cliffs are curved and less challenging as we trace our way back towards the Lodge.

It's been weeks since the hunters last set eyes on me. Since they'd shot at me as I arrived at the iris, the nested islands.

We hear no human sounds. I hope they've stopped looking for me, presuming me dead.

Drelark had consumed the entirety of the hunter who made it to the eye. There's no sign of there having been a search party. They're as disposable as I am.

The forest is confusing, a maze of constantly shifting shadows and vistas. Several times I walk in one direction only to realize I've gotten turned around. If my implant was working, this would be so much easier, but I have no compass, and I don't want to leave any obvious markers as I go.

I must look insane.

My jeans have rips and tears in them, and I've abandoned the useless gun. My thin shirt is ragged, barely covering my chest. Wandering the forest by the light of the moon is dangerous, especially considering there are literal human hunters stalking the woods for prey.

The lodge is only one island away now. The killers are near. I just don't see or hear them.

I clutch at myself, desperate to chase away the chill in my arms. My extremities are the areas feeling the worst of it. I am freezing. It causes me to stumble. The bush that breaks my fall had been shelter to a small flock of ravens and they cry out in alarm before their big wings push them into the air.

"Fuck," I curse under my breath. That hadn't been intentional. Not at all. The chill is making me careless.

I pick myself back up, all on my own, and stumble on. Where is Drelark? What am I doing? How did I think this was a good idea? Good enough to insist on it!

Click.

I freeze. Metal. A gun. Behind me.

"Fucking hell."

The voice is deep, condescending. My heart burns in terror. They've got the drop on me.

My arms are in the air as I turn, cringing at his twisted, grinning face.

"They all figured you'd fell in some hole and died. They're gonna be pissed when I get the kill." He puts his fingers to his mouth and lets out a sharp whistle, summoning either a hunting dog or one of his companions.

This is the point when I envision Drelark coming to my rescue. To see his true, terrifying form lurch from the shadows and disembowel this cocky mother fucker. That vision is supposed to make me feel better, but as my heart lodges in my throat and steals my breath, nothing happens. The world feels so small, just me and the barrel of a gun, a sociopath at the other end of it.

The trees tighten around me, a snare trap.

I'm just a girl. For all my bravado, for all the work I've done to become my own person, it can't change reality.

I can't dodge a bullet from a foot away.

The man wearing camo leers, his beady eyes scanning me. He gestures his gun to get down.

Where is Drelark? This is supposed to be our trap. Our plan!

I drift to the ground, my freezing body trembling with fright.

It's all been a delusion. A hallucination.

Drelark would never leave me to a fate like this, and I haven't seen them since getting to this island, leaving the crater that formed the centre of the eye. Reality crushes in around me, waking me up from my fantasy.

How fucking sad is it that when I'm in a life-or-death situation, *that's* what I conjure up to make me feel better?

What the fuck does it say about me that I fantasized about it making love to me?

"You're in surprisingly good shape for some city bitch that's been wandering the north for weeks." He's impressed, but I feel no pride in his assessment. "Tell you what. I'll cut you some slack. You survived the allotted time after all, right?" he says, every word dripping with malicious intent.

He whistles for his companion again, but the sound is swallowed by gunfire bursts in the distance. His ears perk. His eyes don't leave me.

"Wooo!" Triumphant shouts, another man.

There's no such thing as monsters, Shayde. You've been hallucinating, and now you're caught.

"Get your ass over here, Todd! You'll never believe what I found. Better than whatever you shot."

I can't believe it. I can't believe I'm down on my knees, just accepting my fate. There are a million things I want to do, but my body fails me. I have no weapons, no advantage over them. They found me, their cyber-tech giving them every edge imaginable.

Any fantasy I have of getting out of this alive is just an oasis in the desert. This guy has a good hundred pounds on me, at least. Six-foot even. He's a city guy, but he's big, muscular. Well fed. He probably does one of those stupid sigma training camps that popped up everywhere a few decades back.

My strengths are all in my brain, and that doesn't seem to work great right now.

The moon peeks through the clouds, and he unbuttons his camo vest. His shirt. The gun is pointed at me with the confidence of a man who knows he's already won.

I sob.

He plans to take what he wants. Take me.

I've hallucinated a monster whose organs filled my womb and throat, who is larger and more powerful than this man. I submit to him eagerly, willingly. The thought of this man touching me, though, makes me heave. My entire body trembles. If I hadn't just relieved myself, I'd piss my pants in fear.

"Todd! Get over here. You'll wanna be here for this."

His chest is broad, barrelled, with a soft stomach over hard muscle.

"Shit Gary, I saw something move in the night and..." Todd arrives behind Gary, holding a dead rabbit. At least, I think it's a rabbit. With a gun of his calibre, he's blown most of it away. "Breakfast for the morning!"

He's slow to spot me, but his grin turns wicked as he does.

"Oh hoh, and you got desert."

For weeks I've fought to stay alive, to evade these hunters. Now I've walked right into them, thinking I was springing a trap on them. My brain is so addled from this experience, but the hallucination had been so real.

"Please, I made it past my sentence," I choke out.

Gary and Todd laugh.

"I like a girl who has a strong survival instinct. They're always—" The next word from Todd is a gurgled mess as a sharp javelin pierces his stomach. The shadows shift. It's not a javelin. It's Drelark's tail!

The giant aberration descends from above, obsidian exoskeleton swallowing the light like a void star.

Gary screams, high pitched, terrified.

They can see it.

They can feel it!

A spray of blood mists the air, splattering my face and staining my white top. I don't close my eyes or flinch away. With how hard my heart is beating, I think I might pass out, but adrenaline kicks in and I leap to my feet.

Gary is white with shock, his hairy chest splattered with Todd's blood.

Drelark rips the gun from Todd's hand, and tosses it into the forest.

Gary recovers, lifting his gun with shaky hands.

I grab onto his arm. The trigger is pulled; the bullet arching up into the night sky.

"You fucking bitch! Can't you see what's happening here?!" he bellows. His elbow impacts my chest, knocking the air out of me, but I don't let go. I cling to him, preventing him from aiming a shot at my monster.

The giant being stalks towards us.

Drelark wants to protect me. I'm too close to the hunter. Their claws or tail might hit me by accident, and they're holding back.

"Jesus fucking Christ..." He's breathless, his neck craned back as he stares at the rising figure of the thing I've unleashed.

I release Gary's arm.

Drelark's terrible scream is primal, sounds overlapping each other as various parts of his body join the chorus. My ears ring in pain.

Urine pours down Gary's leg.

His gun is thrown, hitting a tree.

Not just the gun.

No, Gary's entire hand has been severed, ripped away by a single claw. The slice had been so sharp and fast that I heard nothing, saw little more than that.

Gary is slow to notice his stump as blood gushes from it.

He stares at it, unable to believe what he's seeing.

His scream is shrill, but it doesn't hurt my ears like Drelark's cry had. He clutches his forearm, but my monster is not done. The tortoise-shell on their hand cracks open, the tendrils slithering out and into his ear, just as they had done to me.

The hunter goes silent as Drelark plumbs the depths of his mind.

Then, with renewed fury, Drelark roars. Viscous fluid drips from his silvery fangs as he throws the hunter to the ground.

Those claws are sharp enough to rend the man in a split second with ease.

Drelark isn't doing that.

They're gouging the man, but with care, ripping away his clothes. Careful. Meticulous.

The monster had seen inside the hunter's mind, learned what he had intended for me.

They intend to exact revenge for the attempt.

The air is tinged with blood, metallic and sharp. Some part of me, on instinct, roils in terror, but I stare, transfixed. Drelark has power I can only dream of. An extension of my basest parts, the things I wish I could do and can't, and am secretly grateful for. But he has no such reservations, and I don't even know if I can stop him.

If I want to stop him.

I don't.

This man, he's done it before. How could he not? He wasn't nervous, or shocked, or hesitant. He was just pleased, like a man coming home to find a cake for his birthday. There was a certain expectation, and a contentment at those expectations coming to fruition.

My trembling body settles into the soft moss, and I avert my gaze, but I hear every sickening noise. The rhythm of the hunter's heart, spraying more blood into the atmosphere. Some of it mists my face, and I wipe it away like sweat.

The things Drelark does are so precise. So practiced. The way he grips the back of the man's head, and bashes his face into a wood log, just strong enough to break his nose and make a horrid mess, but not enough to end him.

I realize as the monstrous visage of my protector rips away the last of the hunter's camo outfit, that he's using the man's own memories and skills to do this. He's replicating the gruesome, vile actions of a serial rapist and murderer.

Only Drelark does it for justice.

No, scratch that.

They do it for revenge.

They do it for me. Because they know I cannot.

My eyes stare wide in a mix of horror and awe as the terrible violation continues. Gary's body had been so large and imposing, but compared to Drelark, he's small. Delicate. His nudity gives him a certain vulnerability, and he cries and struggles. He finds a branch, and it breaks in his hand.

I wonder if I would have grabbed the same branch.

If I'd have screamed like this.

Despite knowing what a vile man he is, my empathy knows no bounds. I'm sorry for him, for his pain, but I don't stop it.

Drelark's long, pointed tail tip rises in the air.

I flinch away. There's a wet perforation, and Gary screams as the spiked tail penetrates him. It retreats, then thrusts again, and I cover my ears, rocking back and forth.

The screams go silent. There's a heavy thud. The ground rumbles as Drelark tosses him aside.

There's a hole in the centre of him. Guts spill from it.

I'm relieved.

Todd is clutching his stomach as he pulls himself along the forest floor, fleeing.

I'm sickened to enjoy his suffering, to know that some of the pain he's caused to others is being felt by him. Probably for the first time as an adult. It tastes sweet and metallic, tinged with something foul. I stare, but I don't move. I don't have to.

Drelark stomps towards the man, clawed feet cutting through the soft moss.

The whites of Todd's eyes catch the moonlight as they widen in panic, the monster calmly approaching. There's no mercy for him. Not yet. Just as they had for the other hunter, Drelark's unclawed hand sinks into his ears, entering his mind.

His eyes roll back until they're all white.

Drelark beckons me, and I come close. The chill of the night has been chased away by adrenaline, but sweat threatens its return. I close my eyes as they touch me with their other tendrilled hand, their motions tender.

My guardian communes with me in the only way he can, by doing the same.

There's a pinch of pain, then a tickle, as they penetrate my ear again.

Leet stands before me.

"In all my time imprisoned, I was privy to few other conscious presences." He's so calm and civilized, not at all monstrous.

"You were the first whose mind resonated with mine. The wronged. In need of revenge. Not the one who does the wronging," Drelark explains. "They were all minds like this one..."

A flood of memories flash through my brain in quick succession. Todd, hitting his girlfriend. Beating his dog.

Ripping off his own employees, using their pension fund to buy a third vacation home.

When it comes to a memory of Todd going into his own child's room late at night, I recoil and cry out, "Stop!"

The visions end. I recoil and retch.

Todd seems to levitate at Drelark's command, still in his human form. In reality, he must be using his massive arms to lift him.

"There are those who inflict suffering and misery."

Todd screams.

I see nothing being done to him; whatever horrors my protector is unveiling are sealed within Todd's twisted mind.

"There are those who enable the cruel..." Drelark continues coldly.

Todd's nails dig into his own flesh. He claws at himself as if trying to rip something out of his own body.

"And then there is you..." Drelark says, his gaze falling to me.

Todd's suffering takes on a whole new tenor. He ceases to claw and scream, and instead breaks down into pathetic, frightful sobs. Drelark discards him with his gaping stomach wound. His ragged skin.

I've never wanted to see a man suffer like this. The cruelty is too much to bear, the softness in me always searching for the good in everyone else. But I'd seen within his mind, and it was entirely different from my own.

The depths of his masochism I cannot fathom. The view inside his mind was like trying to understand a different species. There was not an ounce of compassion or joy or love within him.

J.M. Keep

This pain pales in comparison to the hurt he's caused over his life.

I hope there is a hell, just so that I can feel like he will *suffer* for what he's done, for at least as long as his suffering resonates on the land. On those he's wronged.

This is what Drelark offers me.

Actual retribution. Knowledge that those he kills *deserve* it, without a doubt. No man has yet found a way to enter into someone's mind, to know the truth as it exists only in the perpetrator's own memories.

There will be no uncertainty, no confusion about whether someone has earned their fate.

I wipe the vomit from my mouth and reveal a smile.

Drelark watches Todd bleed out. He whimpers and sobs pathetically, much like the flicker of a memory I have of his child on his way out of the room. If I survive this, I'll ensure his child knows their father can't hurt them ever again.

This will not be a quick death for him. We are condemning him to die out here from a stomach wound. Every last moment of his sinister life will be in just misery.

"There's still more," Drelark says after a long pause of watching this man experience justice. "Four others. At the lodge. All of them are guilty of heinous cruelty."

He looks off into the distance, towards the location of that hive of evil.

"Four more?"

It's a miracle I lasted as long as I did. I couldn't have done it without Drelark. Without consuming those berries, fruited from their roots.

They saved me from something worse than death. Warmth grows within me. Relief. Certainty.

"Okay. You know the way now?"

I grab Gary's rifle, his severed hand still on the trigger. I shake it off, and it thunks to the mossy ground. The gun is high tech, despite looking antique. These rich pieces of shit can't even go all in on their masturbatory fantasies of the 'good old days'.

"I do." Drelark watches me as I look at the weapon and brings his other shelled hand to my head. More tendrils slither out, the strands entering my ears. He looks like a man, like Leet, but my mind reconciles the image.

Time blurs. Weeks. Months, all in an instant. Rigorous training on how to fire and maintain guns. Memories of the hunters thrust into my mind.

When Drelark ends it, my head is splitting, but I immediately shift how I'm holding the gun, realizing how wrongly I'd been holding it.

"Now you are more than bait too," Drelark says with a warm smile.

"That's a handy trick," I grin. "The government and corporations can never learn about it."

"None shall have it but us, Shayde. Only us."

They lower themself over Todd's body, a claw opening his torso. There is a crack of his ribcage, and then Drelark gorges on his raw flesh.

CHAPTER 15

The wind whips my dark hair behind me. I've never moved so fast in all my life. The trees fade into the horizon as we race through open fields.

My legs wrap around Drelark's abdomen, and I cling to the edge of his chitinous shell.

Four large limbs tear at the ground as he propels us forward. His two smaller hands grasp my waist, the arms double joined.

"Forest ahead."

They are not inside me, and the communication is more distant. An echo across a great chasm, but as long as we're in contact, we can talk. In our own way.

They don't bother showing me a fake version of himself. It would be hard to make my brain process the idea of Leet carrying me on his back like a racing horse.

"I see it," I tell him.

"Duck. Hold tight," comes his voice inside my head. I do as they say.

They lift that big crest upon their head, the obsidian

plate smashing into branches. They crack and break before they can hit me. He may be a monster, but he's my monster, and he looks out for me. Not a single branch so much as scrapes me as he batters through the forest.

It's a rush. I've never been an adrenaline junkie, though I've given it a fair shot in the past. Nothing ever seemed to ignite me when it was taking foolish risks just for a jolt of excitement. Turns out it was the pointlessness of it all. Now there's a reason, and my cheeks are flushed, my heart hammering with the thrill.

We emerge from the copse of trees, only to face a rocky cliff overlooking the lake. We have one more body of water to cross before we're back to where the hunters had their lodge. It's the biggest lake, the deepest. The journey will make us vulnerable to sniper fire.

"What are we going to do?" I ask him.

"Hold tight."

His body moves differently, his back and limbs serpentine as his speed picks up. I cling to him, the gun trapped between our bodies—safety on—and I press myself into him as hard as I can.

We reach the edge of the cliff, and he launches forward like a ballistic missile through the air.

I'm flying.

The world takes on an entirely new appearance with an aerial view. Nature sprawls out below us; the meadows, the forests, the shimmering water. The splendour expands out all around me. Tears prick my eyes, either because of the overwhelming beauty or the bitter wind. In the distance, there is a large animal, watching our arc.

The air is thin, and my heart pounds as we breach the apex and begin to drop.

Land is still in the distance, water black beneath us. We might do it, we just might...

"Hold your breath," he tells me inside my mind. And I do.

None too soon, because when we come down, we fall short of the beach. He crashes into the water with the speed of a torpedo, the motion smooth and powerful. We glide on down under the surface a good ten feet or more until his clawed limbs brush the bottom of the lake.

He seems to take on a new form beneath the water. It's entrancing and horrifying to watch. Bubbles aerate the surrounding water, cracking sounds similar to the roar of groaning ice in his memories. Little wriggling tendrils emerge from him as he rapidly evolves into a new creature.

It lasts only a moment before the tendrils recede and his body becomes sleek. His head elongates on his neck and, like a dolphin, his whole body undulates as he propels himself back upwards.

We emerge from the water much as we entered it: shooting up out several feet, before arcing back down and hitting the ground on all four of his major limbs.

I'm drenched, fear and exhilaration heating my blood as my heart rattles around in my ribs. My stomach finds its way out of my throat and I suck in several breaths before laughter escapes from me.

"You did it!" I say as much as I think, my caution lost because, holy fuck, I'm still alive!

We tread in from the water towards a copse of trees.

Finding shelter is paramount, especially after such an eye-catching stunt.

"We should find a spot and rest until tomorrow night," he tells me as he stalks through the woods. "You need to dry off. And prepare. It will be big. And not without risks."

There's a spot nestled among some old rocks, overshadowed by the forest's canopy. Drelark inspects it before judging it a safe hiding spot for the day.

"Do you think those guys had radio communication back to the lodge? The satellites are fucked and my cybernetics were disabled by the time I woke up here. But they have a lot more high-tech shit."

My words tumble out on top of each other as I catch my breath, still giddy with excitement. The horror of seeing those men eviscerated has been replaced with a sense of power, of justice. The things I struggled all my life to feel even a whiff of.

Drelark helps lift me up off him and place him down, with his third pair of limbs.

"I did not see any such thing on them. Their memories had only short-wave radios."

I giggle, and Drelark tilts his head.

"Sorry, it's just weird to hear you talking about short-wave radios. When you were sent here, they were still using... what was it called?"

"Flag semaphore."

"Right. The original short-wave communication."

They seem amused by my amusement, and their spine tinkle like wind chimes. Withdrawing from my ears, they go to some short trees, and with their claws, they hack some down until there is a bundle of sticks and a pile of leaves.

They find some rocks, and slice up some tinder. While they work, I undress.

My blood-stained tank top goes first, my flesh traced with goosebumps as I remove it from my slender body. I'm not embarrassed that my nipples are so stiff, aroused by the chill and the adrenaline, but they ache and I can't help but notice it.

My jeans are heavy with water, dripping as I strip down. By the time I've undressed and laid my clothes out on a boulder to dry, they have a fire started, a bed a safe distance away.

When I turn to face Drelark again, I'm nude. My slight curves are highlighted by the firelight hitting my glossy skin.

He coils around me protectively. His massive, chitinous forms a shield from the elements, helping bottle the heat onto me. The orange heat radiates onto my bare skin. The chill from the lake is chased away as my flesh dries.

His breathing is a strange rumble, almost a purr. If a giant monstrous creature from some other dimension could purr, that is.

It's far more alien than that, a pleasing rattle with an undercurrent of otherworldliness.

He looks at me with his myriad eyes, and I feel more seen than I ever have before. It's so powerful I'm forced to glance away. I've never felt more naked and vulnerable than I am, reflected hundreds of times over in his compound lenses.

He coils those big, mighty limbs around me. He licks at my neck. The muscle flicks up, touching my ear. Pressing into it.

The familiar lie of his human-like form, so much like Leet, takes hold again.

My feelings shift, and a wave of something pours through me. Pity? That he is so ashamed of what he is. He is glorious, with skills more akin to magic than anything I've ever experienced. But he hides it so that he can be more palatable to the world, to me.

I'm not the same as him, but that impulse to hide who I am, for everyone else's sake, is relatable.

"I don't wish to upset you." He can read my thoughts, feel my emotions. He may not understand them entirely, but he senses the change.

"Nobody ever liked to look upon me. Even when I was tiny."

It was only days ago that I could have understood that. Maybe something snapped in me when we killed the hunters, shifting my terror into awe. When I was small, I had been so scared of dinosaurs, I'd hide my eyes and cry. A kind teacher was patient with me, and as he'd explained why they were so large, how they likely were covered in feathers, how they'd raised their young, I mourned their loss instead.

Now I'm held in the many arms of something that existed out of time with humanity, with power and beauty that I wasn't ready to see.

"I'm ready now," I say out loud, knowing he can feel my thoughts better than I can ever express them.

There was a moment's delay, just a brief pause.

The illusion vanishes.

It is just me and Drelark. My monster.

"I can resume the mask at any time if you grow uncomfortable..." he reassures me. His voice no longer seems to come from his mouth. It is no longer a mouth made for making speech.

The sound of his voice is all in my head, but it seems to emanate from his direction. My mind struggles to make sense of it, but humans are adaptable creatures.

There's a curious tenderness in his words. A vulnerability that is hard to believe comes from this giant killer.

I've always been the outcast. Too thin in school, easily singled out as a scholarship case. My clothes were hand-made. I was too into computers and tech, learning the hardware behind it, why things worked the way they did.

The most unforgivable sin, though, was that I cared too much about things my peers didn't give a shit about. I was never afraid to call out their casual cruelty. Vivian, my girl-friend, was the only one who found me interesting. After I was kicked out—of school, of my home—I thought I'd reached rock bottom, then Aimi was murdered, and I was all alone.

When I first met Leet, I was a bitch to him. All prickly edges, barbed tongue, guarded heart. I wore my trauma and bad attitude like a badge of honour.

It took him years to batter down my defenses, to get me to where I trusted him.

That I slept with him.

I thought Leet was there, at my side, but now I know the truth. With him, I had been more alone than ever.

Drelark is an outcast for obvious reasons, but I'm an outcast for decidedly human ones. We share a kinship, and this time, I don't shrink away from the reality of what he is.

He is as nude as I am, but this is the first time he's allowed himself to be fully exposed.

He lifts his head and inhales my scent, tasting it on his long, serrated tongue. The pause is pregnant, and he leans in. It's as close to a kiss as such mismatched beings as us can share in our true forms. That long tongue slithers along my lips and into my mouth.

His strange hand, with the retractable digits, grasps at my breast, fondling it in a manner that is gentle and yet very peculiar.

He's mimicking human lovemaking, as closely as he can manage. His massive body coils around me, bringing me into him. I'm so much smaller than him, so much more delicate. I hate feeling like this, usually. It's uncomfortable, especially so soon after seeing what Gary had planned for me, the cruelties Todd inflicted. The last thing I want to feel is vulnerable, but Drelark also makes me feel *safe*.

I wasn't even aware you could feel safe and vulnerable at the same time.

A shiver traces down my spine.

I don't shrink away.

Maybe I died weeks ago, and this is some fucked up purgatory. I don't feel quite myself, but the curiosity that always burned in me is an inferno. My fingers trace his shell, over the glossy chitin, and I remember the last time. The glimpses I stole.

This time, I want to see it all. Feel it all. No matter how wrong and fucked up and strange it is.

They have desires, just like me, and I've never been solely attracted to any one gender. I came out as pansexual the moment I first learned the word. Being turned on by a monster stretches the term to its limits.

He can sense my emotions, my curiosity melding with desire. His actions are emboldened. He fondles my breast, taking his tongue from my mouth to slide it on down my body. The ribbed edges tease my flesh. They don't pierce the skin, but excite it.

There's a growing awareness of his abilities that wasn't there before. Just like his compound eyes, I'm reflected back at myself, filtered through his lens.

On my skin, he tastes things about me I would never imagine. My emotional state. Everywhere I'd been. What I'd done.

The serpentine tongue slides around a breast, the tip flicking against my nipple.

I wanted him to do that, but I only realize after it's done. He understands me before I understand myself, peeling back the layers of my psyche.

In return, I sense his interest. The desire to please me.

This is one thing we share in common, other than the need for revenge.

This mimicry of human lovemaking is fascinating to him.

"Your body excites me," he purrs darkly.

I swallow.

Between my thighs, I am wet. He can sense my arousal on the air, on my flesh. In my mind. It's no use trying to deny it. I've completely lost myself to this unearthly beast.

There is a crackling of his hardened hide as it opens below. Their long, horn-like appendage exposes itself. I remember how it filled me, how my pubis bulged as it coiled within me.

My gaze follows his articulated phallus with unabashed interest.

"What is that used for? Usually?"

There's a pause as he considers.

"Nothing," he says simply. "I do not know its purpose. It lay dormant inside me until there was you."

Behind the words, I feel the lack of racial knowledge of his kin. He did not know if he had a kind, or if he was unique. One of a kind.

I like that it's something just for me.

That it didn't have a use before me.

For all my life, I'd known denial, being overlooked. I've never been special, but to him, I'm as wholly unique as he is to me.

"I enjoyed putting it inside of you. Not the same as a human would, but it pleased me nonetheless."

His grip tightens, and his carnal appendage rises between us, a snake charmed.

"Can I touch it?" I ask, my hand trembling as I reach towards it.

"Of course. It awoke just for you. We can learn it together."

His massive form coils around me. His silvery shaft pulsates with excitement as my fingers glide along the prehensile phallus. It is covered in something similar to skin or animal hide, and it is warm. Long, and growing in time with his arousal. It's so alien, and I know it shouldn't arouse me, but it *does*.

His agile, serrated tongue snakes out. It is wet as it coils along my neck, feeling my jugular pulse. It wraps around my throat, constricting. My hand wraps around his shaft. We use equalled pressure to squeeze.

Silver fluid drips from the stinger tip of his phallus.

I trust him.

"You are my mate, Shayde."

CHAPTER 16

I t's a funny word. I remember hearing it once in a show. Not sure if it was British or Australian? Some old slang for friend, but that's not how he means it. He means it in the way that museums and zoos talk about it.

I smile, biting down on the edge of my lip.

His major, clawed arms wrap around me widely. The minor set with the softer 'digits' continues to caress and fondle my body. It's like being held by multiple partners at once, one with exceptionally large arms.

"Do you prefer lovers? I forgot the word love until you came into my radius."

His alien monstrosity pulsates in my hand. His tongue releases my neck, instead licking down my torso. Fanged teeth press into my breast as he pushes me onto my back. His saliva tingles on my skin, the strange tongue lapping at my breast.

"I forgot many things until you came..."

"It all means the same thing," I reply, because it does.

However it is that we communicate, I *know* things intuitively, things I could not guess on my own. It's unbelievably intimate, something I could never attain with another human. Every attempt in my past is a bumbling failure compared to this pure form of connection.

I'm emboldened and I run my hand up the length of his shaft, the sensation strange. It looks sleek to see it, but as my fingers trail along it, it seems to tremble and pulsate. Like a ripple of a wave along its silvery length, it responds to my every touch with such eagerness. It swells sequentially. That's why it felt so good inside me, even though he didn't move his hips or rut in a human way.

"We will right the world together," he says, suckling on my breast. His face doesn't make sense. A great beast with hard ridges, mixed with that of an insect. A stag beetle. To see him mimic that of a nursing child is strangely exhilarating, and that emotion is all he needs to continue doing it. He can't latch with lips, but with his tongue, and the hand with the tendrils massages the other breast, readying it.

He relishes my scent and flavour. His tongue grows until it covers both breasts, squeezing them together with incredible dexterity.

It's terrifying. He could eat me, quite literally, as he ate the hunters before.

He desires to taste my flesh. Again.

But he's committed to not hurting me.

Leet taught me an important lesson. Love isn't safe. Love has to be given recklessly because caution would never allow me to be vulnerable. I could spend all my life building walls around me and die miserable and alone, or I can take a foolish chance at something pure in this fucked up world.

Drelark gives me something more than dangerous love.

My hand wraps around his shaft and it pulsates with intense fascination. We are so different. Our bodies shouldn't even be able to fit together, yet he's better able to respond to my every fleeting desire. I don't need to tell him what to do, because he knows as soon as I do.

It's like making love to a fantasy.

A fantasy that at once meets my every expectation and desire, while also keeping me guessing, utterly surprised by every new detail of his being.

My breasts are raw and sensitive from his rough tongue, and he unfurls his body. His onyx head presses betwixt my legs. A horrifying sight to any normal woman, I'm sure. But...

It feels oh so good when his long tongue begins to taste and explore my slit. The texture of that slick muscle hard to describe; it's the right mix of smooth and contoured, so that my nerve endings sing as he slides along my nether region.

My eyes flutter back and a deep shudder flows through me. I know why he hid his form from me, why he thought I'd always want that. Maybe a normal woman would.

Actually, no, a normal woman would definitely scream in terror and flee.

But Drelark snuck behind all the defenses I'd carefully built. Through my dreams, he found the most intimate part of myself, and showed me something deeper was possible.

Something real.

My lithe body uncoils, my damp skin no longer chilled. A heat builds within me and I moan his name.

He lays me back against him, while his head presses in closer. This tongue thickens towards the base, and while it has those serrated teeth-like appendages, he keeps them retracted. As his tongue slides up inside me, thick as a man's cock, I just feel the pleasing sensation of those ridges rather than the full threat of what they hold.

"You are exquisite..." he rumbles inside my mind. With him inside me, I can hear his thoughts as my own. We are as close as two creatures can be.

I've no choice but to believe him. There's no hint of a lie, and I know I am exquisite as much as he does. I roll my hips, my body moving in time with his as pleasure builds within me. There is still that nagging knowledge of the wrongness of our coupling, but now I embrace it.

My parents were right about me. My rebellious nature pushed everyone away until I was all alone.

And then I found him.

"Right there," I say out loud, though there is no need.

His tongue does a good job of impersonating a human man's cock. He pistons it in and out of me, that dexterous appendage hitting the absolute best spots of my insides. We are two bodies, but one mind in that moment, and he delights in pleasing me as if it were his own pleasure.

His alien hand squeezes my breast tighter, more firmly. The tendrils suction my sensitive nipples. It's so intense I could pass out, but his presence within me keeps me lucid. I borrow from his strength as he feeds that long tongue into me.

I don't last long.

I've been touch starved for weeks, and love starved for my entire existence.

The purity of our coupling is sublime, and I tremble under the weight of it. My hands find a part of him—I'm not sure what with my eyes closed—and I hold on to him as the full breadth of my orgasm crashes upon me.

He teases those ridges on his tongue just enough to turn that orgasm into something explosive. The danger, the excitement, the way it rubs along my sensitive nerve endings... Gods above and below, it makes my body sing.

I buck and thrash. He clamps a clawed hand over my mouth to keep me from screaming into the woods and potentially alerting someone of our presence.

He keeps me suspended in bliss for so long, his tongue working its strange magic until I'm pushing him, trying feebly to make him stop. Only then does he relent, his tongue slithering from my slit, knowing my limit has been met.

"I enjoy doing that to you," he muses.

My brain is a fog, but I know he can feel my emotions. I've never been more alive than I am now. I saved him from a centuries long imprisonment, but he has awakened something potent in me. Something amazing.

My skin glows in the firelight, my pale body flushed with blood.

"Do you want...?"

"I do. I am hungry for you," he confesses readily.

I stare at that organ of his. That masculine appendage, that arose just for me, and me alone. It has not gone down, or away back inside its shell. He caresses me, a hand on my forehead, those strange digits caressing me in his peculiar manner.

I'm not stupid. Tomorrow we're going into a lodge full of people who get their rocks off hunting humans. Hunting young women like myself, raping us, torturing us, killing us, then displaying us as trophies. That's not a place I'm guaranteed to walk out of, even with a monster on my side.

If I'm going to my death, then today, I'm going to experience life.

I'm going to experience something that maybe no other person ever will.

"I want you, Drelark."

He shares in my sentiment.

He uncoils from his spot beneath and around me, and lays me out gently on the bed he made for me. It's such a contrast; his careful actions, his fearsome visage as he looms over me.

This is the stuff of nightmares. Death incarnate in the form of some eldritch being who can never truly understand human life, with scythes for claws, daggers for fangs.

This would undoubtedly scar a normal person's mind for all their life.

But I welcome it, as he poses that silvery member over my slit.

The movement is unnatural, controlled. He rubs his length along my vulva, simulating a human cock from my own memories. Despite being pansexual, I've never made love to someone else with a vagina. Vaguely, I wonder if that's why his body has awoken as it has.

His two large arms keep him suspended from his fists beside my shoulders and head.

There's no impulse for me to turn away or hide within the fantasy he readily offers.

He took the form of Leet, initially, because my heart was still broken. The rage brought us together, and I'm no longer in denial about who Leet is and what he did to me.

Drelark's monstrous form is far more exhilarating than my erstwhile crush.

I rock my hips, my moans held firmly in my mouth, despite how they threaten to spill.

His member is big; bigger than his tongue. Even with his being careful, the feeling of his flared tip stretching me open is a lot to bear. My pink folds are soon ruddy from the strain as he sinks into me.

His tongue presses into my mouth, silencing my scream.

The silvery fluid seems to numb me a little, shrinking the pain as he knots within me. His crown expands, locking himself in place. Even if he wanted to, he couldn't pull out without hurting me. Killing me.

A shudder passes through him as he relishes the moment.

Then it begins.

I stare in awe as his member pulsates.

His girth expands in a wavelike pattern, rocking back and forth. I feel his own pleasure, the sensation of his carnal claim over me. The certainty that I am his mate, the one he's been waiting for since time immemorial.

I gag on his tongue. Another cry of pleasure and pain silenced on him.

Once enough of his length has been fed into me and my pelvic area bulges, his tongue retreats so that I can watch his alien organ. It's hypnotic, like watching waves come to shore before receding. The rhythm is primordial, something older than humanity, and I almost fall into a trance as my body adjusts to the strange sensations.

There's no getting used to this girth, not entirely, but I

become more accustomed to it, and my trembling body grips his chitinous form.

Without the need to move his whole body like a mere human man, Drelark plumbs my depths, and makes me feel the intensity of his lust. That organ pulsates, filling me completely. There is a delicious pang along with the delightful highs of bliss.

Though our bodies are dissimilar, and his desires are not fully knowable to either me or him, there is some latent thread between us. This is a strange new thing for him, but it is tinged with urges to rut and mate. A nature it never discovered until we met.

The primal impulse to breed his mate.

Me.

Leet had used me. Knocked me up despite my insistence on being careful.

Drelark took care of it. Removed it from me in a way that would have been illegal in NV.

My mind and body are frail after this torture on these nested islands. I'm vulnerable like I've never been before. The pleasure I'm experiencing isn't something anyone could ever know of.

I'm forced to drop my gaze as a tremor runs up my spine, and I softly swallow back air. Hot tears bead in the corner of my eyes. This is the finest bliss I've ever known, and I'm terrified of what that means.

Fears of becoming irrevocably bound to this creature become tantalizing promises. The prospect of becoming something other than human beckons me.

Drelark is more than any human man could be. Offers me more than any man could. Why not just accept it?

That thick shaft pulsates and intensifies inside me. The urge to breed has never occurred to him before, but now it's powerful. His emotion fills my mind, the intensity bleeding through the barrier of our individual selves.

He lets loose his strange trill of pleasure as my sex grows dense with his fluid. His seed.

My body quakes as his organ undulates faster, the peaks larger.

I don't shrink away.

Maybe I've totally lost my mind.

I cling to his strange form, not wanting this to stop. Even if it means something unholy. Hell, there's an appeal in that. Of bringing something into the world, born out of a love purer than any social mores could allow. Of loving our child in a way neither of us has known.

I have a rebel heart, and I swallow back a yelp of delight.

This time is different. As the torrential flow of speed spills into me, there is an awareness of life spreading within me. My mind, my essence, unites with Drelark's, and through it, I sense his seed. Just as he was able to communicate with me when I ate the berry fruit of his roots, the connection between us crescendos. Thousands, millions, billions of tiny sparks, seeking purchase within me. They hesitate.

Drelark is not in command of them.

I am.

They respond only to my desires.

I am in control of my body, and of whether I want a child.

His mighty, inhuman form shudders and writhes as his member pulsates. He squeezes at the soft flesh of my chest and backside as he looses ever more of that thick fluid.

I feel myself as he does.

Experience this from his perspective.

Unlike a human who reaches their peak and is done, it is instead a long, quaking bliss that takes hold of him. He savours every moment of our fucking, and his member moves inside of me, able to press and prod my most sensitive bundle of nerves.

He's so large, tied inside my slender body. Pain intertwines with unyielding bliss. My pleasure and pain are shared with him, and his orgasmic heights flood into me.

I'm still sensitive from my earlier orgasm and the sensation of him undulating within me is too much to bear. Quaking, I choke on another scream, my cheeks stained with tears as an intense orgasm grasps me.

I lose track of it all as he shares his bliss with me. Orgasm after orgasm passes through me as he continues to claim me. The flow of his silvery fluid continues until my belly is distended.

By the time we finish, I can barely remember my name. He holds me as the knot loosens, and the extraction is more comfortable this time. My body more resilient. Changed. Adapted.

The flood of that alien fluid is a succour on my tender flesh, flowing along my inner thighs until there is a puddle beneath me.

"There is at least one pleasure in this world beyond vengeance," he tells me, as he coils back around me.

Sometimes his motions, the sounds his body makes, are like a rattling insect, something old that you'd see preserved in stone. It's primordial, his umbral form almost darker than black.

I curl into him, safe. Loved.

"There is," I agree. My voice is hoarse from all the panting and swallowed screams, my throat as raw as the rest of me.

He holds me like no one ever had. Not Vivian, certainly not Leet. We coil into one another, the fire keeping me warm, him keeping me safe and sheltered.

Tomorrow night, we will get my revenge.

CHAPTER 17

I've always been a night owl. I don't know what it is about hackers and just being the opposite of everything society expects of us, but we all share some of the same quirks. Being nocturnal is one of them.

But I'm used to being nocturnal in a city filled with skyscrapers and lights and grinding metal noise at all hours. There was a bodega at the bottom of my apartment complex and it was open 24/7. My building was absolutely crammed full of people, and there was always noise.

Out here it is dark. There are few animal sounds, despite what those old nature docs used to talk about. Every so often there's a shuddering of wings or a far-off scream, but the silence is unsettling. In Drelark's memories, even when this place was nothing but snow, there was more life.

In NV, smog used to blot out the night sky. I'm surprised at how much there is to see when the canopy of trees thins. Guiding lights, however, are not among them. The moon is in its waning period, and the umbral forest swallows what little light it can provide me.

Drelark is more at home in the wilderness, but I can sense his own unease. Things have changed in the time since he was sealed away, and the scars that humanity has left on this once pristine landscape is only known to me through him. Sometimes I can hear his memories of life that filled the arctic tundra, but the last animal I'd seen was that dead rabbit the hunter had, and the deer before it.

I shrink away instinctively as rain falls, and am relieved to find it's not corrosive. In the city, we'd always have to hide under the protective canopies until the rain stopped. There's debate on what chemicals it was that caused it to burn when the heat was just right, but you couldn't argue with reality.

Out here the rain is just... water.

I bring a handful to my mouth and test a sip before taking a bigger gulp.

"We are close. That path."

Drelark motions to it and I squint to make it out through the darkness. The rain clouds have stolen the last light I have, yet my eyes adjust. The land is entirely dark, yet my eyes work as if my technical mods are active again, only better. Crisp. Vibrant.

My implants are disabled, yet my vision is improved.

Am I becoming more like him somehow? An alien in my own world?

The two of us do not belong together in any natural order. And yet...

We walk, hand in hand. Our fingers aren't interlaced, and his clawed palm wraps around mine. It's so natural, although there's nothing natural about it. I smile.

Moving through the brush, I keep the gun close to my

body, feeling confident in my newfound knowledge of how to use it.

True to Drelark's words, the brush is trimmed away, ATV tire marks dug deep into the quickly softening ground. My hair clings to my face and I retrieve my hand from his to push it away, trying to keep it out of my eyes.

My fingers find his arm so we can communicate again.

"I will go in, tell them I won. That they are to bring me home. They'll welcome me in, congratulate me. Pretend they're letting me go. Their defenses will be down and—"

The ground gives out beneath me and I'm falling. One moment I'd been holding onto Drelark's arm, the next, nothing but air.

Pain. Darkness. A scream. Mine?

Then there is nothing.

CHAPTER 18

"Shayde! You made it. I knew you would."

Leet smiles, his angular face stretched into an unfamiliar expression. He's dressed in a suit, a fur cloak wrapped around his shoulders. The lodge is warm, lit by a fire, and he's bathed in a golden light.

Where is everyone else? Why is he alone?

"You fucking didn't know I'd make it," I cry out, running towards him. I slap him, hard, the sting of my palm jerking his head to the side. He smiles still.

"Why would I send you here if I wasn't confident that you'd return home to me? This was the only way, pet. The only way I could get the Corp off your back. They were on to you long before you confessed to me, don't you see?"

My anger waivers and I take a step back. My boot squishes, mud at the bottom of my sole. The puddle at my feet grows as my clothes drip with rain water.

"You're lying."

"Of course not." He takes a step towards me, reaches for my face and I shrink away. My eyes narrow in rage.

"Shayde, don't be like this. You're always looking for the worst in people, but you know me."

"I thought I did!"

"You do. You're the only woman I ever let myself get close to. The rest of those bitches, well, you know how they are. Always self absorbed, just interested in their own vapid bullshit. But you're different, Shayde. You're special."

I suck in air as I come back to consciousness, staring up at the rain clouds as they pelt me from above. Shadows move at the entrance of the hole, but I'm uncertain if it's Drelark or just the trees rustling in the wind.

Touching my temple, my fingertips are coated with inky black blood and I groan.

I'm so close to the hunting lodge. I can't give up now.

My legs are shaky and I push my hand into the mud wall as I stand. The pit is about ten-feet deep. I explore it with my hands, quickly finding that there are many spikes lining the edges, and more beneath me. The only thing that saved me from death was the detritus from the forest floor that had grown thick enough to outmatch the spikes. This must have been here for a long time, because some of the wood spikes are rotting.

I won't be able to climb them without risking falling back again, and this time impaling myself.

The pit was probably twenty feet deep. Even with Drelark's size, he couldn't just reach down and grab me. Without our physical connection, I can't speak with them, and I don't want to make a noise, lest I alert the hunters.

Then again, would they be out in the rain? Those pampered sociopaths don't strike me as the type to want to get messy.

Not in any way that wasn't violent, at least.

The soil and debris beneath me are turning to thick sludge, and the filthy water is rising fast. It's nearly at my hips. If the rain holds, I'm going to drown in here. One of the rotted spikes juts out just above my knee, and I test my weight on it. It's sturdy enough. I grab for the next, just in time for the one beneath my foot to loosen, and I lose my footing.

I'm too weak. I can't hold on. My arm gives way and I splash back down into the soupy water.

"Drelark!"

Nothing. He's silent. He's severed the umbilical cord to the nature of this land. I can't hear him, and I'm uncertain he can hear me. He knows I'm down here, but with how fast the water is rising, I don't have time to wait for him to save his damsel.

I have to free myself, so I find another spike, but this one slicks out of the mud with a light touch.

A shock of light jolts against the sky. Seconds later the silence of the forest is split by a boom of rolling thunder. I'm jumpy and grab for my gun, but it didn't make it down here with me. At least, it's not at the bottom of the pit. I look upwards, hoping that another lightning bolt will illuminate it.

It's only a split second, but it's enough to illuminate the angelic halo of a woman's golden hair as she looks down upon me.

CHAPTER 19

"Oh my, you poor thing! You're lucky I came by."

She has a syrupy sweet voice, and even in the pitch black and the rain, she is radiant. She seems to emit her own light, or maybe that's just because I'm so fucking grateful for her serendipitous arrival.

"Hey! Can you help me out? The water..." I wipe my hand against my face, clearing it of the rain for half a second before more gets in my eyes.

"Here darlin', I got a rope. Watch your head. I don't wanna whip ya or nothin'," she replies, and a second later, a thick coil topples over the edge of the trap. There are knots in it every foot or so, and I grab onto it. Sturdy. Must be tied to a tree or something.

I pull myself up, only to be sucked back down. The mud is too flush with liquid, and it's gripping me like a predator. My arms are weak, my body famished and emaciated from my time on this gods forsaken prison island. I sob, my entire form racked with the intensity of it.

"It's okay, take a deep breath. Don't panic, alright? Your boot stuck? Here's what you wanna do. Wiggle a little, yea, just like that. Good girl. See how it's makin' a space for you now? That's what you want. There you go. There..."

Is she some new-age type out here for a nature retreat?

I climb the rope the second time, and there's less pressure around me. I make it up a foot, then another, until I'm above the water.

Her hand is so soft. She takes mine, and she helps me up the rest of the way. I lay back on the ground, catching my breath as she kneels next to me.

"You got lucky, sugar."

"Tell me about it," I groan, pushing myself up. My white tank top is soaked with mud, torn in multiple places, and my jeans weigh at least twenty pounds. I'm exhausted, but now that I'm free, reality comes crashing back down on me.

"We gotta get out of here," I say, pushing myself to my feet. "Do you have supplies? A boat?" I swoon. When I fell, I had hit my head, and pain radiates from the wound. My vision blurs. I wipe the rain from them, but it doesn't help.

The woman reaches out for me, keeps me on my feet.

"Be careful, sugar. Don't want you to fall back in."

She's about the same height as me, short, and she hides her ample curves beneath a baby pink raincoat. Her eyes are a golden brown and even in the darkness, they have a faint glow to them. Implants, probably.

My head throbs. Am I concussed? How do I know?

"Yea. Yea, we gotta go though. The hunters. They'll be here soon."

"The hunters?"

Fuck, she really doesn't know. This poor woman. Why the hell is she wandering around out here in the dark? My stomach churns and I almost lose my balance again. Buckling over, I vomit, and I try to convince myself the dark specs aren't blood. I'm no medic, but head wound and throwing up blood isn't a great combination.

"There's a lodge. They don't just hunt animals. They're looking for me. We need to go."

"Oh sugar, you really hit your head, huh? Come with me. I'm just over this way, and I'll get you patched right up."

"Okay, but then we gotta go," I murmur, consciousness bleeding away from me. She smiles at me, I think, but the darkness is so thick I can almost feel it wrapping around me. I'm so woozy.

"Why are you out in the dark? And the rain? Aren't you afraid?"

"More stuff'll kill you in the cities than out here, hon, what with all the gangs and the minorities."

My spine stiffens in warning, and I fall back a half step behind her. She takes my arm, guiding me forward, down the ATV trail. I can't expect the woman who rescued me to have perfect politics. But why would she say that to me? Why would she think I'd agree?

Sure, my cybernetic implants are discrete. She probably can't smell the city living off me, especially with my clothes caked with mud. But even in this darkness, there's no way she can't tell I'm Asian.

"How can you even see?"

"I live out here. My great-great-granddaddy was real smart. He knew the end times were upon us, so he brought us all up here. I know this place like better than anyone."

The back of my neck prickles as the hairs stand at attention.

No. No, this isn't good.

I look around, but I may as well have my eyes closed for all I can see. The motion of my head causes me to stumble as the world spins, and she grips me tighter.

"Careful sugar. Almost home. There," she says as the trees clear and some lights sparkle in the distance. Smoke from a fire lifts into the sky, blending with the rain clouds.

My blood turns to ice.

Umbridge Lodge.

Chapter 20

"**N**o!" I pull my arm, but am unable to break her grasp. She's surprisingly strong for a woman, and her grip tightens on me. Her manicured nails dig into the soft flesh of my underarm.

"Come on, sugar. It's warm and dry and, oh, so cozy."

"You're Patrice Umbridge! Fuck, I should've known. There are no photos of you."

"Of course not! It's Umbridge and *Sons*, darlin'. The men in my family know how to protect their women. And the women know how to be modest. Somethin' you might want to look into."

She doesn't even glance at me to prove her point. I can feel the tears in my shirt, know my skin is bare. My tits aren't exposed, but they might as well be with how frayed the fabric is. Instinctively, I bring an arm 'round myself as she continues to tug me through the mud.

The storm is letting up, and the warm lights of the lodge could almost be mistaken for homey. I know what's inside, though, and the acid in my stomach churns.

"Why don't you just kill me?" My voice is stringy and desperate, so different from the casual-cool tough-girl vibe I refined back in the city.

"Well, you been here, what? Thirty-nine days? We all been figurin' a mountain lion got to ya first! I mean, that's a record 'round these parts, sugar! And *that's* something worth boasting about."

The trophies flash into my mind. She's not talking about *me* boasting about surviving so long. I stop dead in my trail and Patrice lets out an admonishing sigh. Thirty-nine days. It didn't feel that long, but this is one thing I do not need to question Patrice on. Why would she lie about that, of all things?

"Come on now. Let's get you back home. I'll draw you a nice bath, get you all cleaned up. We just got a shipment of new bath oils. It's made from a whale they thought extinct, so it's a real treat. Could be the last of its kind! But I'll share it with you, if you come with me peaceably."

An icy shiver goes through me as cold gun metal presses into the base of my spine.

Of course an Umbridge child would be carrying heat. If I hadn't hit my head so hard, I would have known better than to trust anyone on this island, woman or not. A gun to my back robs me of any last ounce of agency.

I walk on. She doesn't need to finish the threat. My knees tremble and bile rises in my throat. The lights are on in the lodge, the gaudy windows tinted to give the people inside privacy. They can see out, but nothing can see in. Even on a secluded island, the Umbridge family is secretive.

The large wooden double-doors open. She glows in the radiant light, and I see her clearly.

Her skin is porcelain and almost as smooth. Her honey eyes do, indeed, have cybernetic implants, likely giving her dark vision, maybe even heat vision. They have a metallic sparkle to them, and shimmer as the electronics spin. She's recording me.

"After you, sugar. Make sure to take your boots off at the door. I don't know how you animals do it where you come from, but out here, we're civilized. We do things the proper way. You'll need to strip down, too. I don't want you trackin' in all that mud."

I've been defeated.

Where is Drelark? Why haven't they returned for me? Did they go to find supplies to rescue me and get captured?

I take off my soaking boots, placing them neatly on the weaved doormat. My socks drip as I pull them off. It's hard to remove my tattered tank top, and it rips as I try to pull it over my head, so I just add it to the pile.

Last are my jeans, heavy with mud, and I fold them, placing them atop my boots.

Naked and vulnerable, I follow Patrice up the grand staircase. My gaze stays locked on the honey-maple hardwood floors, unwilling to look upon those grotesque human trophies again. We're in a different part of the lodge, and there's a strange scent in the air. Almost sulfuric. It fizzes in my nose unpleasantly, and I'm grateful when she leads me to a bathroom and closes the door behind us.

"Just us girls," she says.

The bathroom is unreal. Luxury that doesn't belong in a wood lodge, even one this nice. The room is bigger than my first apartment. The floor is a solid block of white marble, and it is seamlessly carved upwards to form the bathtub. It must have been one massive piece when they brought it in. I can't even imagine how much it cost.

But despite how much it must have cost, it's cold and clinical. There's no beauty to be found in it.

True to her word, she draws a bath, taking out a blue glass vial and dripping some oil into the water. Steam rises, and despite myself, I long for the warmth. My body shivers, damp and nude, and I remember Drelark's body wrapped around me. He felt so safe, like the answer to all my prayers.

For the first time since he spoke to me, there's an absence, a gnawing lack. He severed his connection to the land, and now I can't speak to him. Even in dreams. Not without him being physical present.

Patrice tests the water. Her clothes are completely dry, same as her hair. I don't understand how. We've only been inside a few minutes, haven't we?

"There we go. Perfect. Get on in. I'll grab you some-thin' for your head. And I know I don't need to say anything, but I do feel it's my duty to remind you not to do anything silly, alright? Brother has eyes all over the house, especially in the bathrooms and bedrooms. That's where sin lives, after all."

She smiles as I try to cover myself again.

"Good girl. Modesty is what sets us apart from the animals. Get on in under the bubbles, and I'll be back in two shakes of a lamb's tail!"

I hate that I let out a pleasured sigh as I submerse myself into the water. I sob, but tears refuse to fall. Dehydration has me desiccated, and this bath is like a last supper for someone on death row. A thing I find enjoyable twisted about into a sick pantomime of itself, a ritual on the march towards my end.

I sink down into it, the expensive oils luxurious on my thinned skin. The bottle likely cost more than I've ever made in my life, and Patrice taking such pride in the fact that it came from an extinct animal sends vibrations of inept rage through me.

She's just like Todd. There's no humanity in her. Instead, she lusts for the suffering of others, feels satisfaction in pain that is not hers. How are we even the same species? I've never realized the depths of cruelty, even when I was forced to stare it in its face after Kyoto fell.

Resignation seeps into my pores, and I dip my head under the surface. My hair floats up, the wound on the back of my head stings. My fingertips gently clear it of debris. A scab has already formed, so that's good.

I laugh.

A hysterical, ugly thing, manic and wild. Tears sting my eyes and still refuse to fall.

I'm going to die and I'm relieved that my head wound is healing nicely.

I should have stayed in that cave with Drelark.

Revenge isn't for people like me. Justice isn't for people like me. It's an illusion, the carrot before you get the stick. The Umbridge family has been refining their own version of justice in this lodge for decades, this island better fortified than most prisons.

I swallow back my laughter and focus on my breathing.

I was dead the second I trusted Leet.

Everything since that moment has just been an inevitable death march.

How had I been so naïve? In him, I saw someone living my childhood dream. I really thought he was trying to take them down from the inside. Someone compassionate and kind, wearing the mask of indifference just to disarm our enemies.

There are no windows in the room, just the sink, a toilet, and several blindingly white towels. There are no potential weapons, not unless I get really good at garrotting someone with a bath towel.

Too bad Drelark didn't upload that into my brain.

But he gave me other information. Well, Todd did, when Drelark linked our minds together.

About the guns, sure, but also... I know this place. The layout of the lodge. At least part of it.

There was literally no information about this lodge that I'd found in all my research on the Umbridge family holdings, and certainly no floor plan. Drelark's mind connection thing is the only way I could know the layout of this place. Even though I can't speak to him, he's helping me. I can't let him down.

This bathroom is above the kitchen.

Todd waited outside the kitchen door and raped a servant as she exited. The memory makes me sick, but I force myself to look at it. Study it. She'd run inside, and he'd followed. She took a right, and there was a staircase. The same one Patrice led me up. He'd dragged her back to the kitchen.

When I visit the memory, I can feel his emotions. His amusement at her trying to get away, how he wanted her to struggle more. I feel them as he felt them, and rage boils my blood as I'm forced to look at life through the eyes of a sociopath.

Don't think about it any more. Just remember the layout. If I can get down the stairs before Patrice returns, I might have a chance.

The cameras are, of course, an issue. Patrice likely has full access to the security feed with her implant, and she'll be watching me. It's humiliating to dwell on, considering my little manic break. Hopefully, the blank expression I wore throughout school is still keeping my thoughts hidden right now.

There is one option.

I don't really like it, but maybe...

"She in there now?"

I startle, splashing water onto the marble floor. A man is right outside the door. I hadn't even heard anything until he spoke. How good is the soundproofing in this place?

"Yes, Brother. I'm getting her all cleaned up for you. A few little cuts and scrapes but nothin' that will scar once I get the ointment on her. Oh, you're gonna flip your lid when you see her, Nate. She looks like one of those dyin' orphans the way her skin is just fallin' off her. So scrawny."

Patrice's saccharine voice is poisonous, and I dip down in the water as if I can hide from her. What the fuck is she talking about? Looking down at my body as it distorts under the water, my ribs are poking out, my hip bones pronounced. My skin has an uncharacteristic elasticity, the skin almost translucent. I watch a blue vein thrum with the rhythm of my heart.

She has a point. My skin looks like it was made for a woman bigger than myself. Despite never being a healthy size, I've wasted away. The deer cooked in acid is the most

I've eaten in almost six weeks, and with all the travel, it barely helped.

But what's that have to do with anything?

There's the sound of a parting kiss, and then nothing. Silence. I know she's on the other side of the door, so what is she waiting for? I stare up at the ceiling light, still covering myself as best I can. My gaze is hard, my jaw set, and I win our imaginary stand-off when she enters.

Her smile doesn't crinkle her eyes or brow, and she's changed. A blue polka-dot dress, cinched in the waist with a white ribbon. Her hair is coiffed in careful curls, and she's wearing fresh lipstick and mascara.

She reminds me of a sex doll. Perfect, but in an uncanny valley way. I look at her carefully as she leans down and offers me some unmarked white pills.

"You have the aura of someone who did a stint in an asylum, am I wrong?"

She's not, and I hate her for saying it. My jaw tightens, and she holds out a glass of water. The exterior is sweating with condensation, ice rattling inside.

"Good. Then you know the drill. Pop the pills, then say 'ah'."

Sex dolls are really well made, generally.

It started as just programming people's minds, but humans are notoriously fragile, so those with cash to burn wanted more 'robust' models. Something that can take more punishment. Still with a human body, a modified human mind, but with more cybernetic implants than a normal person could take. It's all about getting them when they're young.

But this is Patrice Umbridge. The odds of them modifying one of their own?

Well... not unheard of. There was a president in the former United States whose sister was lobotomized for being too annoying. Technology and science have advanced a lot since then.

I pop the pill. Cheek the pill. Drink the water. Open my mouth. Lift my tongue. She is satisfied.

At least the psych ward was good for one thing.

"Now to take care of those owwies." She pulls a tube from the apron of her dress, squeezing some ointment onto her fingertip. I flinch, but she rubs it on my temple, at the back of my head, my shoulder. My flesh knits back together with an uncomfortable itch, but she bats my hand away when I go to scratch it.

"I don't know how you all live without this. A miracle drug," she informs me proudly. "My daddy always knew the value of using real test subjects, but did you know the government wouldn't allow that before he showed them the way?"

There'd been some rumours I'd stumbled on about a human trial for some designer cosmetic drugs, a bunch of deaths, but it was all speculation. Patrice is getting way too comfortable confessing shit she shouldn't with me. She's talking to a dead girl, as far as she's concerned.

But I'm not talking to a girl at all. She's a facsimile, something so close so as to almost be indistinguishable. It's only my experience with cybernetic implants that gives me the eye to see what others wouldn't.

I sit up in the tub.

"Is there soap?"

"Of course there is! I'm so proud. You know, cleanliness is what sets us apart from the animals."

Her dainty hand grabs the bar of soap from next to the perfumed oil, and as she turns back towards me, my fingers tangle into the back of her perfect hair. My grip tightens and I slam her head down onto the sharp edge of the marble bathtub.

She tries to shriek. I use every ounce of strength I have to pull her down towards me again, her jaw impacting on the marble. I jerk away as a tooth projectiles through the water, striking my thigh. The bottom of the tub is slippery and I use the wall to break my fall. Blood spills into the water, mingling with the oils to turn it a foamy pink. I spit out the pill, and it sinks in its protective casing.

Patrice twitches, then goes still.

I don't have much time. Drelark said there were four other hunters at the lodge, and he didn't know about Patrice. Clearly, this family has secrets that even the other fucked up sociopaths here don't know about.

I'm stark naked and I'm not going back for my clothes. Instead, I begin to unzip Patrice's dress. She groans, and I back away. It's not worth it.

The adrenaline and a hunter's stolen memory are all I can rely upon.

I will not fucking die in this gods damned lodge.

CHAPTER 21

The lodge is quiet, but I know that doesn't mean it's empty. The soundproofing is unreal. The only reason I could hear in the bathroom seems to have been the fact that the marble is slightly recessed from the door for drainage. Other than that, this place is sealed up like a rapist serial killer's wet dream.

The exact location of this island eludes me, but meeting Patrice filled in some blanks on what fucked up cosplay they're running out here. Generations of doomsday preppers turned arms dealers. With so much wealth they're barely even human. Nothing but poor imitations following a script from a past that never existed.

But at least Nate isn't waiting outside the door for me. Downstairs, I hear the crackling fire. I should have grabbed a towel. Patrice groans again, and I don't waste another moment.

My footprints are damp until I reach the bottom of the stairs, but just to be safe, I beeline away from the servant's kitchen. If anyone's watching the cameras, hopefully they'll be heading in the wrong direction. The first door I test is locked, but the second one slowly turns in my hand. I push inside, and my insides instantly revolt.

Not only is this place soundproof, but there must be some industrial strength odour suppression technology at play. The scent of viscera and gore and shit fills my entire body, a taint that I'll never feel fully clean of. Even just that moment before I shut the door again has permeated my flesh, and I scurry away.

I hesitate at the next door, but when I enter, I'm relieved to find it's just an office. It's a place to rest, to hide for thirty seconds—long enough for the cameras to catch me—before I rush to the kitchen. Bookshelves line the walls, all leather tomes, some new, but many looking decades or centuries old. It's the kind of place I'd have loved to explore, but today is just about survival.

There are no weapons mounted on the walls. Maybe there's something in the desk?

I step forward, and the early morning light filters in towards a recessed corner of the room. It must be a trick of the eyes. The taxidermy animal in the corner is large and imposing, and at first, I thought it was a bear. Then I see the wings.

Leathery, thick wings spread out from the beast, and as my gaze rises, the face twists into an unnatural contortion. It's not a bear. Its face is too flat, too hairless. The eyes are a strange bluish purple, like a galaxy marble. Fangs protrude from its mouth, and they still seem to drip with blood, the light glinting off it in just the right way to make it look fresh.

My quest for a weapon is forgotten. I turn, running to

the kitchen, and I don't stop until I'm out the door, gulping in fresh air. Reflexively, I bat away black flies. There are none. Some tech keeps them at bay, I bet.

The morning is overcast with an unpleasant chill. I wish I'd stayed in the bath longer, enjoyed it more, but it was a deadly mirage. I know that. Still, as my bare feet sink into the muddy ground, a girl's allowed a fantasy.

Patrice referred to the Lodge as home, so I imagine she lived her year-round.

The hunters, however, come and go. Todd spent more money than I've ever had on a ticket out here, promised the hunt of a lifetime. He came in from the city, though the memories about how he got here are hazy. We weren't connected long enough for me to fully experience his entire life, but helicopter or boat is my best guess.

That leaves a limited time frame for my escape. Not to mention having to do some hostage taking of the pilot or captain or whatever.

I'll figure it out when the time comes.

For now, I have to focus on finding Drelark.

It's been hours since I last saw him. Was he captured as well? Would Patrice have been alone in the woods to find me? Or did they just send her because they knew I'd be more likely to trust another woman as an ally?

This fucking place is one of death and decay. The rotting stench still stings my lungs, and the misty air can only dilute it so fast.

There's a building a few yards away. It almost disappears into the surroundings, the natural logs stacked in an A-frame. Firewood is pressed up against its side, large antlers hung above the double-wide doors.

It's a lot older than the main lodge. Maybe it predates the cameras?

My bare feet are instantly covered in muck, the comforting scent of the lavish oils diminishing with each step. Being naked is horrible, and I'm terrified not just of the men hunting me, but also of more mundane threats. Finding a patch of poison ivy would suck, or even falling on a twig. I should've taken the time to kill Patrice, taken her dress. At least that'd be something.

But I pity her. She's a victim too, in her own way. Implanted with god only knows what kinds of tech to make her docile and submissive. I couldn't kill her. I'm not like them.

The clouds are still thick and angry, the air pressure heavy. The wood door creaks as I open it. Dry heat washes out, tingling my skin. My mouth waters at the scent of tender meat. Row upon row of large cuts of game meat are hung, the smokehouse unlocking a primal urge in me to consume. I'm so hungry, my body is wasting away.

I subsisted on berries and mushrooms for weeks, but the last few days, I've been ravenous. My body cries out for meat in a way I've never felt before.

A quick scan of the room shows no visible cameras, not that I can trust there aren't any. They've gotten so discreet they could be hidden in even a small knot of wood, but with the heat and the smoke, I doubt there are eyes in here.

I lean against the rough bark of the wall, catching my breath. Each inhale makes my stomach rumble with need, and I move through the rows of meat in a daze. The silver scales of a fish catch my eye, and I reach out, tugging it off its hook.

It could've been here a day or a week, and I can't say if it's safe to eat. But I've been starving for too long, and without food, real food, I haven't got a chance. Worst that could happen is I get sick and vomit, and then I'm right back where I started.

My teeth sink into it and I moan. Saliva practically runs down my chin as I take bite after bite of the best fish I've ever tasted. It's moist and flavourful, pleasantly falling apart in my mouth. Grease stains my cheeks, puffed up like a chipmunk hoarding for winter.

The last time I had fish it tasted like cardboard, dry and white and chewy. This is a bright pink, bordering on red, and the taste is divine.

I discard the bones as I come to them, spitting them onto the dirt floor before gorging myself again.

My eyes drift heavenward.

Instead, I see hell.

CHAPTER 22

The metal fish hook in my hand thuds to the ground.

Above me, there are a dozen people. But not all of them. It's people's skin, strung up and tanning like leather. Their arms and legs are splayed, tied taut on carefully manufactured frames, and there's no mistaking it. One has a tattoo with the name Casey in a heart. Another has genitals still hanging limp between their legs.

Even when I close my eyes, I can still see it, smell it in my nose. The fish hasn't even made it to my stomach, and it's threatening to come back up. Despite the heat of the smokehouse, my skin turns to ice, sweat beading down it as I turn and bolt.

Thud.

I wasn't looking at where I was going, and when I open my eyes, a beautiful face wears a facsimile of a smile.

"Eager beaver," he says, his tone mellifluous, thick and warm like dripping blood.

I jerk away from his hand as it wraps around my bicep,

and he doesn't flinch. There's no urgency to catch me, and he simply observes as one does a bird with clipped wings.

"You're lucky, you know. This island offers something you city girls rarely taste. Purification." He tilts his head, examining me to see if I understand. I'm an animal to him, something inhuman, and my expression disappoints his appraising gaze.

He sighs.

I'm just a dumb animal. How can he expect me to understand?

"It's a compliment, you know? You made it almost a month and a half. That's something to be proud of! You're almost as pure as me now. The taint of the city still clings to your muscles and tissue, of course, but this cleansing period was a gift."

He laughs, the sound rising like heat from a volcano until it spills from his lips.

He's tall, six foot or so, and built like a college athlete. A thick head of blonde hair and unnervingly clear blue eyes. I've seen a dozen guys like him in glossy magazines selling expensive trips to the great outdoors.

But I've seen him, specifically, on the Umbridge and Son's website.

Nathanial Beauregard Umbridge the Third. Current CMO of Umbridge and Son's. The public face of the company. He could pass for a man in his mid-twenties, but he's actually pushing forty.

Patrice called him Nate. Her brother.

The door is still open behind him and I bolt, only for a thin wire to wrap around my throat. I gag, instantly falling back a step to avoid garrotting myself. The wire goes lax; he has a fucking animal catch pole around my neck, and he holds the rod casually as he moves towards me.

The smell of meat is so thick in the air now, choking me. It's not all animals. There are humans in here. Hung on hooks. Aging like beef. His gaze is flaying me alive, moving up and down my naked skin. I tremble and he shushes me.

"Perfect. No tattoos. Not even any scars, except for these ones." His thumb moves over my wrist, his flesh warm and soft against my pulse. The old scars are a reminder of my painful past, and I hate him seeing them.

"The hands come off anyway, don't worry. They're too tricky to use for much aside from soap or as offal for the dogs. Impressive for being in the forest as long as you have been. This place is untamed. But then, there used to be wild horses until we broke them."

He stares off wistfully.

The smoked fish churns in my stomach and I swallow back my vomit.

He bends down, inspecting my thighs, and I glance towards the door. Morning light burns away some of the fog as the sun rises. The lodge was built in the most hospitable portion of the island. The weather is much milder and less oppressive here.

Still no sign of Drelark.

The caustic stench of death surrounds me.

"My sister took good care to clean you up for me, and you went and got all dirty again, though. Tut, tut. I'll have to speak to her about that. Even still, I have to say, Shayanne, Leonard was right about you. You *are* a fine piece of ass. Don't worry."

He's using my real name. Leet's real name. They're like

acid on his tongue. My eyes narrow in rage as Nate stands to his full towering height, giving me that same manikin smile.

"I promised Leonard a taste, so you'll always be a part of him. He told me how important you are to him. And now that you're cleansed of the taint of the city, you will be sweeter in death than you were in life."

He lifts my damp hair off my shoulders gingerly, almost tenderly, and I shudder. My muscles are knotted like frayed rope, and his finger traces down my spine. The snare hangs around my neck, lax, but still a threat.

Patrice's blue polka-dot dress dances in my peripheral vision.

She's not dead. Of course not. A high-end sex doll is built to take a beating. I'd hoped I'd injured her enough to escape, though.

"Your skin is practically falling off you with your weight loss," Nate says, knelt down to my hip level. "That will make it a lot easier. I can't believe my luck. It's been years since I've had a specimen so fine. Those damn hunters have no appreciation for what it is on offer here. They're hardly better than you, all base urges—"

Nate begins to stand. I'd been a trembling hunk of live-stock for him, so he's not expecting as my body loosens all its tension at once. My entire weight falls forward in a dead drop.

The snare tightens around my neck, slicing into the skin, then releases as I hit the dirt ground. I've taken Nate by surprise, and he topples forward on top of me.

His knees land hard on the back of my shins and I cry out. There's a sickening thud of flesh hitting metal, and he coughs and sputters. Rolling onto my back, he's holding onto his throat as his blue eyes water.

The end of the animal catch had stopped his fall, right on his Adam's apple.

No time to celebrate.

As his face turns red from rage and pain, he lunges forward towards me. I scramble backwards, right into Patrice's stockinged legs. Nate charges like a bull, and with all that momentum, he can't stop himself at the sight of his sister's maimed face. Blood drips from her gaping mouth, the sinew of her cheek muscles barely holding onto her jaw. Viscera splatters on my forehead as Nate's fist misses me and instead lands in his sister's gut.

She buckles forward, wheezing, splattering more gore over my naked body and Nate's formerly pristine beige sweater.

"You fucking bitch!" he howls, his voice raspy after the impact on his throat. Meat shlicks from their hooks with a sickening wet sound before thudding to the ground. "I'm offering you immortality! Better than an animal like you deserves!"

I dodge his next blow, and Patrice's throat produces a guttural suspiration of anguish.

"What did you do to my sister?"

I've seen monsters. Drelark terrified me with his chitinous form, the staccato chittering sounds he makes, the alien way he moves. The trip into the hunter's mind, the evil I've seen from the perpetrator's own eyes, will haunt me forever.

But the way Nate transformed from a cool, detached psycho into the man standing before me now shatters a part of my brain. The fact that I've hurt Patrice has unleashed something horrifying. All his talk about preserving my beautiful skin is off the table. If he flays me alive and drinks my blood, that won't be enough to quench the rage exploding within him.

I leap to my feet and dive towards the work bench. A cattle prod rests in the nook beneath it, and I grab it, whipping around to face him. He catches it with ease, and I'm no match for him in raw strength. He pushes me back, back towards the tanning racks with the human flesh strung taut on bone frames.

I wrestle for the cattle prod, tears stinging my eyes as the stench of smoked human flesh burns into my nostrils. With a firm push, he sends me to the ground, his form towering over me. My hand lands on the fish hook I'd dropped earlier. He's too blinded by rage to notice, and my fingers tighten around the end.

"You don't deserve immortality," he snarls, bloody spittle dripping from his full lips. "I'm going to cut off your head, and I will fuck it in every orifice until the skin melts from your skull."

CHAPTER 23

The fish hook sinks into Nate's genitals.

A jolt of pain consumes me, the cattle prod sparking on my skin.

My vision fades, along with my other senses, and I lay there as an ungodly amount of electricity dances on my bones. The world goes dark, then rushes back in vibrant reds. Meat. Skin. Blood. Gore.

Nate clutches his genitals, the fish hook still protruding from his pelvis. The end sticks up, pantomiming an erection, bobbing as he flails in pain. Patrice has rushed to her brother, and is trying to soothe him in that honied voice, but her jaw swings limply beneath her skull.

I lunge forward, grabbing the hilt of the hook, and yank it out. A spray of blood covers me as I bring the hook up towards his face, the sharp hook skewering his mouth shut. Yanking it back, it takes his cheeks with it.

The siblings have a strong familial resemblance now. Their lower jaws dangle precariously on stretched sinew.

Except Patrice's jaw is tightening. Some scientific

miracle is involved in producing a doll of Patrice's calibre, and I watch in horror as her skin begins to knit itself back together.

My head down, I charge forward, and my skull makes impact with Patrice's soft stomach. There's a clatter of metal, thuds of meat hitting the ground in my wake. She crashes into the wood door with a sickening crack of bone, and behind me, Nate lets out an animal cry.

I turn just in time to see him jump to tackle me.

I brace for an impact that never comes.

A noxious smell fills the air as blackish sludge oozes from a wound in Nate's stomach. The end of a spit pokes through, and behind him, an ominous black shadow rises like the grim reaper.

"Drelark!"

My heart seizes, skipping irregularly before finding a rapid rhythm. I still can't hear him, not his words at least, but a tiny gesture in one of his tendrils is enough. I dodge out of the way as Drelark pushes not a spit, but his tail, forward, goring Patrice on the other end.

The brother and sister are forced into a bloody embrace as Drelark impales them both. Their mutilated faces can form no language, but for the gurgling death that bubbles in their throats.

We both stare, watching the blood and viscera pool beneath them. I step away as it drenches the earth, the heinous scent of shit and innards making me gag.

The terrifying monster before me looks ferocious.

My saviour.

He waves the two siblings around like some giant, human-kabob that is at once both grotesque and darkly comedic. I laugh at their miserable fate as he batters them to the walls, punishing his skewered toys.

Drelark lets out a strange, terrifying rasp and cry as he takes a hold of the brother's head with those strange hands that let him pry into minds. He then bears his fangs in a terrifying manner as he lets loose an awful screech of rage.

He knows what was done to me.

What the true monster had intended to do to me.

Drelark rips Patrice from his tail and tosses her aside like a discarded piece of spoiled meat.

Nate screams in anguish as Drelark pries him off his hooked tail, the spiked segments tearing at his insides along the way.

Drelark throws Nate onto the workbench. His dagger-like claws find purchase in Nate's flesh, and he begins to peel the skin from the muscle. It is calculated, practiced. Drelark has stolen Nate's memory, and is using the man's own talents to flay him alive.

Nate's cries send a frisson up my naked arms.

Teary eyes distort the scene, and though it's horrible, I can't look away.

The skins in the back, those were people. Humans like me, who had been punished by being sent to this island to be tortured and killed.

Maybe this will give their souls some peace. I don't really know. I'm just compelled to bear witness to their suffering, reflected upon their tormentor.

My atoms will remember their pain. Their vengeance.

Long, agonizing minutes pass. Drelark is methodical, and he is drawing this out. Just as Nate had. With his flesh partially removed, he's unable to move, but still, he screams and sobs.

Drelark's claws are especially sharp, and his skill and dexterity are unmatched.

The brother's heart beats still as he lays there, largely skinless. Muscle and tissue are exposed as blood smears and pools along the workbench, dripping onto the floor. He hiccoughs his breaths, twitching and shaking.

Drelark looms over him and licks the fresh blood straight from its source.

The brother cringes with some of the last energy in his body.

Drelark rises and abruptly lunges towards me. His shelled hand opens, the tendrils finding purchase in my ear canal once more. I lean into it, eager for the connection.

"I lost you! Could not find you! They lured me into a trap as I searched," he rages, furious at his own inability to save me.

My arms wrap around the hard shell of his body as I weep, my naked body covered in mud and human excrement. Most of it not my own.

"You need to find a way out. He'll know one. Before he dies," I plead, fighting the urge to just run into the forest and cry.

His mighty, terrifying limbs wrap around me. He holds me, and I feel more secure than I have any right to feel in this circumstance. An alien take on a hug. An embrace.

When at last I calm, my tremors fading, Drelark turns to the flayed body of Nathanial Beauregard Umbridge the Third. They slide a slithering set of fingers into his orifices.

The look of pain and discomfort on the dying man's face is palpable.

I relish it.

It disgusts me.

My eyes roll back into my head as Drelark opens my mind. I'm flooded with the memories of a devil who once wore the skin of a man.

Death still stalks the forests.

CHAPTER 24

The hunter crouches low, gun in hand, as he moves through the brush of the northern landscape. He's stealthy, experienced; he's hunted for many years.

None of that will save him.

Drelark is too fast. Too much of a natural born killer.

In the moonlit night, Drelark rushes through the fields, his long, obsidian form glinting in the silvery light. It's eerie how quiet he is as he moves. How nearly invisible he is if you don't know to look for him.

He's closing the gap on the hunter, who, though armed, has yet to detect him.

Tension fills the air for me, as I watch this all play out from a thicket atop a hillock. I'm so distant to it all, requiring a scope to even see these details.

Drelark is closing in. The gap narrows.

A strange rhythmic beating sound thrums overhead in the distance.

I glance up and see a dark helicopter.

Someone is coming.

And we haven't yet dealt with the remaining hunters.

I have to focus. One thing at a time.

The helicopter bypasses us, en route to the Lodge. It will have to wait.

Drelark is just about there. His thickest limbs tear up the earth with the increased urgency.

He leaps, and a crackle of energy bursts out from the ground, blinding me. I have to squint and take my eye from the scope, rubbing it. When I look back, the hunter is grinning, gun pointed at Drelark.

My monster is penned in by fiery-blue pillars, imprisoned once more.

The horrible shriek Drelark sends up splits the night, reality tearing along the edges. My heart races, wishing I could do something as the hunter taunts him. Minutes pass as I sit there, useless.

I've hacked into the hunter's comm system, and I wait. The notice crackles in my earpiece.

"I trapped it. Whatever this thing is, it's like nothing we've ever hunted before. Nothing we've ever seen before!"

There's no response. Silence from the hunter's companions.

Twenty minutes pass as Drelark paces his enclosure, a zoo animal wearing grooves in the dirt.

Are the others coming? I know they're out here. I'm about ready to call the plan a wash when I spot another hunter, grinning as he high fives the other man.

They gloat over Drelark's captured form. A monster in a cage. Their comfort with being so near him makes me uneasy, and empathetic pain floods me.

Luckily, I don't have to see it much longer.

Our bait worked, that's what's important.

I squeeze the trigger.

The first hunter's head explodes with bloody gore.

With reflexes I didn't know I had, I fast move to line up a shot with the other hunter, and fire.

Fuck!

The tough guy shit was an act. He's jumpy in the presence of a creature like Drelark, and he bolts. My bullet misses his chest, tearing through his arm. It dangles from his shoulder, bouncing as he runs. He finds tree cover before my next shot can make its mark.

"Fuck," I curse out loud. Jumping to my feet, I cart my rifle and race down the hillock towards the pen and the forest beyond. I can't take down Drelark's cell and catch the hunter. As hard as it is, I sprint past my mate and stay on the hunter's trail.

The islands are more familiar now. Not just because I spent the last six weeks of my life being hunted on them, but through Drelark's strange magic. Nate's memories, glimpses of things, knowledge.

It didn't come perfectly contained and refined, but an assortment of odd things that I don't see the connection between until I need them.

There are traps all over, like the one that caught me. I know where to avoid, the little tells of disturbed earth or uneven terrain to look for. It's become an instinct, something known in my bones, and I'm thankful as I dodge aside just as a snare lifts into the air. My hair whooshes up with the rope, but I'm still free.

The hunter screams, panicked and pained, so he makes

for easier prey, but nothing about this is easy. The woods are thick and dark, even in broad daylight, and it eats up sound with a greedy hunger.

There's blood on the leaves. An arm dangling from his side will gush mass amounts, and to a trained eye—or at least, my stolen awareness—it's easy to follow. It looks strangely dark and eye catching in the night.

Beautiful.

The brush ahead of me rustles, and I duck just in time. A shot splits the air. No birds cry in alarm. No animals scream. The world belongs to humanity, and still the hunters thirst for more death.

The hunter has staunched the bleeding, found some tourniquet. He's still gravely wounded, and crawling through the forest to get away.

I have the advantage.

I also have patience.

For six weeks I've waited for this moment. I will not fuck it up by getting premature about things.

My slender body is hidden in stolen camo gear, and my hair is pulled back from my face. I take slow, deep breaths as I lift the heavy gun, but my arms don't tremble. There's not an ounce of pity or hesitation left in me.

When I woke up and realized I was prey to some human hunting party, I knew they didn't deserve compassion. After what Drelark showed me of their minds, I know they don't deserve a painless death.

But there'll be more now, so call it a mercy.

His back is against a tree trunk after towing himself across the ground. He holds out a handgun with his one good arm, shakily pointing it about, unsure of where I might come from. He's on a hair trigger though, and even with bad aim, he might hit me. The forest doesn't favour sniping. There are too many obstacles and obstructions.

I'm small. Light. Sure-footed. Each step is intentional. My heel digs into the dirt, then slowly the ball of my foot rolls forward. The leaves don't crunch. No twig snaps. My breath is high in my chest; in through the nose, out through the mouth.

Don't make a sound.

Almost there.

Another foot. Another. Another.

I can almost reach out and touch him.

He jerks his arm in my direction and fires multiple wild shots.

One tears through the sleeve of my stolen camo top as I dive behind a tree.

A quick check shows I've shed no blood; it didn't hit me. But it was still way too close for comfort. From my pocket, I grab the tool they used to distract their prey. A fidget toy with a light. Simple, but effective. I toss it off to the other side from beyond my tree, and it draws his fire.

I seize the opportunity.

With one more squeeze of the trigger, I blow off his other hand.

He is left with a stump and a handless arm as he screams into the night.

I'm not a sadist, but my newfound skills were inherited from one. Maybe that's why I don't take the easy shot for his chest. Some instinct to toy with my prey.

It's discomforting, and I just want him to stop screaming. To put an end to that awful wail of anguish. I aim higher.

My gaze is stolen further upwards. A shimmering spectrum of colours dance in the sky, and the breathtaking display nearly brings me to my knees.

The man twitches in pain, disarmed—literally.

I look at the hunter, my eyes narrowed. A torrent of blood pours from his stub, rolling down one of the broad leaves towards the forest floor. The mushrooms will feast. Life, fed by death.

"Don't. Don't," he pleads, falling to his knees. "I'll pay you. You win, you win!" He presses his bleeding wrist into his thigh, desperate to staunch the bleeding. It blossoms out on the fabric like an inkblot flower, the red almost black, glistening in the shimmering light-show above us.

He hasn't noticed it at all. I can't blame him, I guess, but I'm having a hard time focusing on anything else. In the city, there was no sky. No stars. They were all just stories that I couldn't tell apart from a fairy tale.

The northern lights were more mythological than factual.

I gesture up. His face warps in confusion, but he follows my gaze, then looks at me, incredulous.

"What? You want me to pray?" His laugh turns to a barking cough and he spits. Pushing himself up with his bloody stump, he's unsteady on his feet. "How much to let me walk, huh? You'll be set for life. There's a penthouse on the east coast I own; can't rent it out at what it's worth. Just been sitting vacant for years. It's yours. View of the Miskatonic River."

"This isn't a negotiation."

"Cunts like you always pretend like it can't be bought, but that's because you lack imagination."

Above me, greens and purples and reds undulate, and awe fills me. He is untouched.

How are we even the same species?

I lift my gun and take aim. He stares defiantly.

"There are monsters in this forest, girl. Without me, what do you think they'll do to you?" His grin is contemptuous, a warped sneer.

"Without you, there'll be one less monster."

Pop.

Pop.

It's such a small noise, so harmless, but for the fact that a split second later, his eyeballs explode in gore. First one, then the other. The bullets strike the tree behind him and it quivers. Pinecones bounce from his head before he collapses unceremoniously on the forest floor.

There's no time to gloat. Drelark is waiting for me. I need to free him, and make sure we commandeer that helicopter before anything more happens. As I move, my gaze keeps rising to the heavens, the majesty of this natural phenomenon spiritually stirring.

I force myself to hurry. Drelark was caged for decades, and it must be traumatic to be trapped again. The lights above me dim, and I focus on the path ahead. Once I free him, we'll just have one more issue to take care of and—

Pain, agony.

It arcs through my whole body as I tense up, lose all ability to move.

Down I go.

Awareness fades to black.

CHAPTER 25

I awake back at the lodge.

Is it? What is that fetid stench?

My head is splitting, my vision slow to come unblurred.

This is not the austere decoration of the lodge, that ultra modern simplicity.

No, this place is ancient. Aberrant. Strange symbols adorn the dark walls, written in blood.

A throne built from skulls.

More hold candles, emitting an unnatural red light. Others form ghastly adornments. Strange, ghoulish decorations made of human bones at an altar of evil.

A metallic scent in the air mingles with decay; old decay. It's earthy and bordering on pleasant, but tinged with death. My skin prickles with an awareness my mind hasn't yet fully comprehended, but I know that this place is wrong. Unnatural.

I reach for my gun. It's not there.

Instead, I get a slap across my face, sending me reeling.

I'm slow to recover, looking up to see a tall man in a uniform. A flash flood of memories hits me like another jolt of electricity stronger than the cattle prod.

Time bleeds. The present melts into the past, and the earthy scent gives way to the sterile bleach of the airport. Everything is so white it's almost blinding, and my vision clouds over.

"Turn around. Bend over. Part your cheeks."

I comply, staring at the poster on the wall, talking about terrorism and the signs to watch for. The airport security agent sticks a camera up my ass. I grunt.

"Hey, be grateful. At least you've got your freedom." My cheeks burn with rage, but I bid myself to remain docile. This is my only chance at getting out of NV. Starting shit with security before I board my plane is a fast way to get thrown in prison on terrorism charges. With my expulsion record, I'd be totally fucked.

"Alright, turn around." The man is red faced, sweating in the heat of the airport. The sun beats in through the black paint they used to cover the windows. They originally wanted to replace the windows with shaded solar panels, but the city went with the cheapest bid, so this is what we got.

"Squat."

I do so. Other passengers make their way through security, white faces being waved through. My indignity is on full display, but it's so routine that they don't even notice.

"Okay, this might pinch."

Another device enters my sex, and the pinch is no pinch. I cry out, biting down on my lip as the security officer glowers. It hurts more, and he stares into my eyes, watching the tears pool on the surface. I don't let them fall, and eventually, he relents.

"She's clean," he says, waving me through. I pull up my pants, grab my luggage, and rush into the boarding zone.

I'm in a daze as I take a seat, and hours tick by. Finally, I decide to call Aimi.

She's barely answered when I burst into tears.

"They delayed the flight again. I'm never going to get out of this fucking city," I sob.

The airport is half abandoned. The 'do not fly' list has grown again, and the list of no-fly zones along with it. Japan is still technically with the Alliance Forces, colloquially known as the Eumaricans, so it's basically the only place I can go where I know anyone.

"Shayanne, don't worry. You'll be here soon, and it'll be a fresh start."

Through my stormy eyes, my cousin Aimi is a bright ray of sunshine. She's in her late twenties, a decade older than me, but has a natural maternal aura to her. When she found out my parents kicked me out and I was couch surfing, she gave me an out.

I didn't take her up on it 'til Vivian, my girlfriend, broke my heart.

It was the streets or Japan.

I chose Japan.

Now if only my flight would board.

Swiping my tears, I sniffle, an ugly, phlegmy sound. Aimi doesn't flinch.

"Yea. I've waited six months for the travel permit. I can wait a few more hours."

It's about as optimistic as I get these days. A forced

smile saps my energy, and I slump down in the rusted metal chair. "What's the weather like there?"

"Not a cloud in the sky," she smiles, happy at my lame attempt to rebound. "What about there?"

"No clouds. Or maybe it is all clouds. Hard to tell with the smog."

"Even around the airport?"

I glance out the window, seeing a monochromatic tarmac.

"Yup. Probably why flights are always delayed."

"Well, I'm going to make you some *Sakana no Nitsuke* when you get in." Aimi places the phone down and I stare up at her ceiling. When she comes back on camera, she's wearing an emerald green peacoat and a matching hat and mask.

"I'm going to head to the store for the ingredients, and I'll bring you with me so you can see your new neighbourhood."

This time, I don't have to fake my smile. The streets are clean, and the sky is so blue it almost hurts to look at, even through the screen. She pans the view over her front yard, across the pink petals of a tree in bloom.

"This is your yard?"

"Yes. My garden," the video reveals a series of carefully manicured bushes, and several flowers swaying in the breeze.

"You'll have to teach me."

"I'd be honoured to be your teacher! And the shops are just this way," she says as she walks, pausing to greet a neighbour along the route. I don't understand what they're talking about, but fruit is offered and accepted. People move casually through the street, their clothes breezy, no gas masks or bulletproof vests in sight.

It's jarring, like walking through a VR simulation of the past. My heart aches with longing. I can't wait to join her and start again. Kyoto was occupied as the former states broke out into civil war. There were already military bases nearby, and they mobilized fast. The city was spared a lot of destruction once the Japanese government capitulated to the army's demands.

Being a puppet state is better than being target practice for the West.

"Ah, looks like the clouds are rolling in," I note with a sigh. "With my luck, it'll be raining acid when I land."

"Now boarding for Kyoto, Japan." The announcement startles me to my feet and I'm just about to tell Aimi goodbye when I hear the screams. Not from the airport. From the idyllic community I'd just been living vicariously in.

"That's not—"

The call drops.

I board the plane, and we sit on the tarmac. There are others trying to reach family in Kyoto. None of us can get through. The plane stays grounded. Hours pass. I watch the smog turn dark with night.

No answer.

Maybe the satellites are down again.

No answer.

Maybe there's debris in the atmosphere again.

No answer.

Maybe...

No.

"The Euro-American Alliance General LeMay joins us now, live, with news from Japan. General, thanks for joining us."

His face flickers on the tiny tv, each seat lighting up with a crackle. Greens bleed into reds until his skin looks like flesh and his dark eyes stare into my soul through the screen. His head is blocky, his voice gruff and dispassionate. He reads from a script without emotion or connection to the words.

"Tonight, a traitorous enemy breached the missile shield that protected our erstwhile ally of Japan. Nuclear bombs were released simultaneously across many cities. All report that they have been utterly destroyed. This shows the importance of keeping the faith, and never abandoning our military commitment to one another. The people of Japan are paying a heavy price for demanding an end to the Alliance. One I hope the rest of our citizens can learn from."

"And what of our men, General?"

The man smiles, his eyes catching the light in a twinkle. Pride radiates in his otherwise dispassionate tone.

"I had ordered the withdrawal of our forces earlier in the day. We suffered no losses."

"Well, it sounds like we got very lucky to avoid any loss of life! Thank you for joining us, General LeMay. After the break, we have tips for how you and your family can save money by replacing Prat meat with Mearita's newest product, Proffal!"

Stepping off the plane, I'm in a daze. I keep asking my cybernetic implant for information, but it repeats the

General's statement over and over again. His words become etched upon the tissue of my brain.

"What happened to Kyoto?"

It's an impulse. I can't help myself.

This time, the message is different. My cybernetic implants flash a warning on the back of my retinas.

"Warning. This information is confidential. Please continue to the nearest militia detachment for interrogation. If you do not comply, a retrieval vehicle will be dispatched. Your expected arrival is in one hour and twenty-two minutes."

I stop walking, and a man bumps into me. He regards me with disgust, suspicion. Paranoia builds within me.

I remember little of the following days or weeks. Months in an asylum blurred together with routine, but every time I closed my eyes, I saw her face. His face.

I'd thought it was clouds coming in, but it was annihilation. Aimi. Her neighbours. The glimpse of a peaceful existence. It was all snuffed out.

It broke me.

Half a year passed before I was released from the psychiatric unit. I was monitored for several months after. I found a job as tech support for a company selling cybernetic implants. That's where I met Leet. He vouched for me, got me off the terrorist watch list.

By that point, everyone but the most stalwart of Alliance defenders would admit the truth.

The General had punished Japan for withdrawing from the war.

Millions died, simply to send a message. To show that he could.

It's been a decade since then, but he hasn't changed. His waxy skin is thick on his broad face, his lips fleshy and too wet, a fishy pucker.

There's no screen between us this time, and I'm frozen in the past, trembling in fear. Warmth spreads between my thighs, ammonia stinging my nose as I lose control over my bladder. The personification of evil manifests before my eyes.

CHAPTER 26

The beating surpasses pain.

Every inch of me is battered and bruised, but I'm numb.

There is only so much a person can take before the pain fades into noise. My cries of pain and anguish have died down. That pisses him off. He liked my screams. Enjoyed knowing the power he has over me.

I take smug satisfaction in it.

One guard hands the General their knife.

My body betrays me, quaking on the altar of death.

"Where are the boys? Tell me now, you mongrel cunt!"

Spittle strikes my face, stings where the skin has been split. I can see the knife from between my swollen eyes.

I had been so close to triumphing. I only had to get back and free Drelark...

Now there's no part of me that remains untouched.

Blood cakes my face, some of it dry, some of it sticky on its way to drying.

I'm aware of these things, but it isn't me.

I float above my body, a dispassionate observer.

The woman on the wood table is so small and frail, her face barely recognizable as a person anymore. Purples give way to yellow; reds that look almost black in the eerie light. The shack stinks of excrement and death, the skulls surrounding the girl like a promise. Empty eyes and slack jaws gawk at her, bearing witness to the crimes enacted upon her body.

I watch too. She cries, and I wish I could wipe her tears away, but I can't. My role is not to interfere. I am a bystander, as helpless as the skulls I sit between.

Even if I knew where the boys were, well enough to describe it, I wouldn't. She wouldn't want me to, so I'll hold her secret deep in a place where this monster can't get it. My hand rests upon a skull. I'm not sure if it's a human's or an animal's. I stroke its smooth surface and hope that it is comforted, all the same.

It's how I distract myself as he puts that blade into the eye socket. There's an awful, wet sound of flesh and blood as he pries the eyeball out. The socket suffuses with blood, and the ridges form a crater around a newly formed lake in my skull.

He's shouting something again, but I can't make out the words anymore. Too far gone for that.

I'm halfway to becoming a skull, just like the others. It's fascinating, this transformation. The becoming. There's so much blood. Red light from the candles flickers, high-lighting the liquid as it spurts from the girl's empty cavity.

The barbarous General has done this before. There's no shock or awe, no appreciation for the absolute power of destruction he wields. Millions have died because of him, but not all have been as indirect as a nuke.

His anger is apoplectic, but there's no lust or satiation for his work.

No artistry either.

His words foam into each other, waves crashing along the sea shelf.

He fades into the black, and everything becomes very soft around the edges. There's a crackle of fire, a patter of rain, wind through the trees. The universal vale dips around me, calling me down below.

I smile as I sink into the ground, bringing my skull comrades with me as we curl into the warm womb of the earth.

CHAPTER 27

A ring of pure agony bores into my skull from that place that had once been my eye.

I reach a hand to it, find some gauze stuffed in there.

He must want to spare me, to do more damage when I'm awake to feel it. My other eye is bloodshot, a film of red laid over the world. He's not over me right now, not next to me. I can hear him breathing, or something breathing. The altar grows unearthly warm beneath me. It seems to breathe, too.

Is this a hallucination?

Can there be so much pain?

My ears pain as a loud sound echoes around me. I lift my head. The world spins.

There's a chain of cacophonous shots; fully automatic bursts. Then screams.

I dip back for a moment, woozy, when the doors open. The General is sweaty, panting. Two of his men fire shots off wildly. The muzzle flares of their guns lighting the darkness in a strange, film-like quality.

He pushes the door shut with his two arms, heaving all his strength into that old, heavy barrier.

I slip my legs over the side of the sacrificial slab I'm on, and slowly sink to the floor. My body is unsteady, my shins and thighs worked over with metal rods. There's no place that isn't bruised, and the muscles scream as I force myself to stand.

The General grabs a beam, barricading the door. It won't last long. The knife he'd used to tear out my eye sits, unmonitored, behind him.

My hand is bloody. All of me is probably bloody. My palm is sticky with it, and when I grab the hilt, it fuses to my flesh. Becomes an extension of my arm, just as that inky club had back in that field.

There's not a single part of me that doesn't hurt, but in the edges of my vision, I see cherry blossoms. Bright, fresh. A promise that never came to pass because of this man. An aura of death clings to him, but as my light footsteps press into the dirt ground, he can't sense his own end is nigh.

When I told Leet about my cousin, about this man, he feigned sympathy. I was so ready to believe it, because I couldn't understand that a person could *know* what this man did and not feel the collective pain and suffering of humanity.

I saw this man as an aberration.

The easiest person in the world to hate.

My nostrils flare, the scent of his fear thick in the air.

"Has he ever felt fear before?"

My voice is so distant, I'm not sure if I say the words or just think them, until the General turns and faces me.

He's pushing three-hundred pounds, his tall body broad and stocky. He towers over me, but he bled me of life, and with it went my sense of self-preservation.

The calm of the earth still lives in my heart, and I observe him impassively.

I hope there is a hell, because if I had a hundred years, I could not show him the horror he's perpetrated upon others. All I can do is try to put an end to his terror before he ends me.

A frenzied mad woman out of some man's nightmare, I charge. My grin is feral as I lunge, knife and nails brandished. He tries to block my assault. The blade slices through his forearm, rending his muscle. My nails are sharp and claw his face.

He punches my ribs, but I can't feel it. I'm beyond pain. Physical limitations no longer exist. I have become death. I've died and been reborn as a spectre of righteous vengeance, my ugly feelings purified in blood. The knife slices into his torso, under his arm. Skin flops away from itself. I dodge his grasp, my motions erratic.

The knife sinks into his bicep, and I turn the hilt. He screams, spit flying. His uninjured arm reaches for the handgun on his hip. I slash out just as splinters of wood explode behind him. His large body shields me from the shrapnel as Drelark's giant hand bursts through the door.

My hero.

My monster.

A claw the size of a short sword pierces through the

General's arm. It dangles uselessly; the gun fumbles to the ground.

His blood stinks like bile, the poison of his heart pumping hard as the door cracks inwards. Drelark pushes into the room with a spray of blood, re-birthed with a baleful cry that shakes the foundation of the forest.

We fall into a visceral dance of carnage with the General as our guest of honour. My love and I are reunited in the gore.

I press the knife into his meaty thigh. The blade is so sharp; I don't stop until it strikes bone. There's a terrible scraping sound, and I hear the screams of destruction echoing in my head.

"We suffered no losses."

It's been a decade, but the words repeat, just as clearly as they had that day on the tarmac.

Aimi's neighbour smiles. She's in her eighties, wearing a white scarf. She's offering Aimi some fresh oranges. Wrinkles of countless joyful moments are etched into her face, reminders of a long and happy life.

The mushroom cloud looms above her.

I remove the blade from the General's leg. A spray of blood gushes from it, painting my legs. The General grabs my head in his massive hand, thumb threatening my good eye. A crackling scream splits the air as Drelark bellows, and the General covers his ears in pain. He buckles over, and Drelark's tail lashes forward, whipping around the General's throat. It constricts, the tiny barbs bringing pinpricks of blood to the surface.

The man hovers in the air, dangling from the neck. His legs kick as Drelark's multifaceted eyes observe me. They tremble in rage at my state, frozen in empathy for their mate.

Their spines prickle with untold anger. Their cry distorts my vision, and veins bulge at the General's temples.

I rush in at the offered hangman, but a foot thrusts out. It catches me in the guts and I drop to the dirt floor.

Can't breathe.

My eye waters. My eye socket cries bloody tears. Drelark rends the General's arm, and with a sickening crack of bones, it falls to the floor. I slash out, dragging the blade along the man's inner thighs, lacerating his femoral vein.

His blood falls like pink flower petals. Time slows, and my head tilts. I smile.

A fresh start.

Drelark rips off his other arm, holding it high in his massive, clawed hand. He slams it into the man's guts, winding him, just as he'd winded me. His spittle is stained red now. I dig the knife into his side, dragging it along until his intestines spill out, first slow, then fast as the weight pulls them down.

The stench is overwhelming, and though I can't hear his scream, I can see them etched into his face. It turns purple. His breath is held in his torso as Drelark's barbed tail tightens. He bucks and twitches, but Drelark does not allow him to die.

Claws and knife and nails gore him. Our audience of skulls demands more. I can hear the cacophonous thirst for vengeance rising in this sacrilege place. So much pain and suffering. How much can one cabin in the woods bear, all because of one man?

His ante mortem moments are defined by suffering,

and it can never equal that which he wrought on others. I hope that if there is such a thing as a soul, his victims can know an ounce of peace as his death throes pass way to stillness.

By the time we're done, the General is little more than a pile of goo. His remains sink into the Earth, feeding the dead below. Blood covers the skulls, returning them to vitality.

It feels wrong to return him to the cycle of life and death, as if his taint might continue to spread even from beyond. The poison of his cruelty should be purged from the material plane.

But in death, he is equal to all that has come before, and all that will come after.

My puffy face aches and sears as I smile. Wounds in the process of closing coming open again. My arms are too sore to lift, but Drelark embraces me, and I collapse into his preternatural form. He doesn't speak, but I can feel his rage, his pain. It radiates off of him, a soothing vibration of energy. I relax, knowing that the injustices enacted against me have been felt, known by something outside of myself. I don't have to carry it all alone.

The aches dull, and this time, I'm within my body. Drelark gives me a sense of safety and home that I've never had before, and despite how battered I am, the soiled state of my clothes and body, I relax.

My impulse is to explain. Who the General is. Who he was. Why I killed him without mercy, torturing him until there was nothing left of him to torture.

I don't need to.

Drelark's connection with me removes the need to

revisit those awful memories and experiences, because he simply *knows*. He feels it as deeply as I do.

He is my mate, and I am his.

Silence reigns as the candles burn low and then, one by one, they snuff themselves out on the rising wax. Darkness embraces us both, and when I stir from an unknowing slumber, there's a strange sensation. I feel it in under my skin, and it's not the pain. It's something alien. New.

"We should head back to the Lodge," I say to Drelark, stroking his bestial face with the back of my fingers. "Justice will not wait long. If word of Nate gets out, this place will be swarmed with mercs."

"We will be ready for whoever comes next. Not like this time," Drelark says as he cradles me.

I pick up the General's head, his eyes unblinking, unknowing. His spinal column sways beneath it, the sticky viscera dripping into the puddle of carnage at my feet.

Was he sweet, once? Was there love in him? It doesn't matter any more.

My remaining eye is still swollen, but I stare at him and wonder at the fragility of even a monster like him. They are not invincible.

They just want the world to believe they are.

But the monsters of men are still mortals, and I've just claimed their deadly game for myself.

The rules can stay the same. If they survive a week on the island, I'll let them go, the same way they honoured those words with me.

I grab the gun and tuck the General's head beneath my arm.

I'm coming for you, Leet.

CHAPTER 28

Flesh, my flesh, has begun to knit back together.

When I move an arm, it doesn't pain.

My face is no longer as swollen.

I had thought of getting an artificial eye; they come with neat tricks nowadays.

I don't need it.

A new eye has sprouted in my socket. My vision is beyond my imagining, and my brain is rewiring itself to understand. This is how Drelark sees the world. It's not yet full size, but every day, it grows.

There's something inhuman about me. A corruption of Drelark and I's mating? It doesn't feel like a corrupting agent, though. It feels like I'm being reborn as something new. Something special.

Something powerful.

Drelark's ability to plunder the minds of the men paid off.

We have a plan now.

A good plan.

At first, I thought we would use the knowledge Drelark had to dismantle the companies.

The complexity of the Umbridge & Sons operation is beyond anything I'd expected. If we made an obvious move, they'd cut out the men we assumed the identity of before any damage was done, son be damned. Nate had fallen out of his father's good graces years ago, and his father is itching for an excuse to disown him.

Too much wealth rests on the companies being greedy forever. Always expanding profits. A half-percentage point loss and there would be a purge of anyone tied to those decisions.

There is no ethical way to dismantle this company.

It is a parasite, and all it can do is feed. Grow.

The war machine is its most reliable source of sustenance.

I mourn the girl I was before all this. The one who thought there was a chance of taking them down from the inside, or of doing one brave, foolish thing, and slaughtering the war pigs.

She was so sweet. The idea that someone could *actually* be evil was unthinkable to her, once upon a time. But that was all a fairy-tale.

A weak hope to subdue riots.

I have to be realistic now.

We can't go back to NV. One glimpse of Drelark and the drones and bombs would rain down on us. There's only one place left for us.

Here.

From the Lodge, we can call them to us. Lure as many

hunters to us as possible, promising them the hunt of a life-time. Something they'll never forget.

One by one, we could chew through some of the world's most powerful, evil men.

But there was one man we would start with. One very important man.

Drelark and I lay on our backs, staring up at the sky. The stars flicker in the chilly night air.

There's a new moon tonight. A fresh start.

A fresh start.

CHAPTER 29

Dear Leonard Reymond,
  Mr. Umbridge is extending you a personal invitation to the island to thank you for providing us such a challenging hunt. The chopper will be ready to receive you at the following date and time.

  We look forward to your visit, Mr. Reymond.

  Sincerely,

  X

THE LODGE IS MASSIVE. I keep getting lost in the hallways; the soundproofing swallows my footsteps as I wind my way deeper into the belly. The perimeter is lined with windows, but the interior is cavernous. Austere interior design leaves little clues about where I am, so I have to rely on muscle memory to find the dining room.

It's been over a week since we laid claim to Umbridge Lodge and all the disgusting and dangerous secrets it contains.

The dining room is one of the few rooms with any personal touches. Cold metal and rock and wood gives way to the warmth of a fireplace. I've already set the table in the gold and silver dining set, and crystal glasses glitter in the midday sun.

I haven't yet dressed for dinner. The idea of cosplaying in Patrice's trad wife shit sickens me.

The Island is empty except for us. I've gotten a lot more comfortable in a casual nudity. Especially since my body was so sore after the General's brutality that even the idea of clothing caused me to wince.

My bruises have faded, and my body has grown softer. I've not been able to trust the meat in the smokehouse, but I can't let it go to waste. Drelark has been consuming the red meat. I've devoured more fish than I ever dreamed possible.

The kitchen is well stocked. Last night, I made us *Sakana no Nitsuke.*

It was divine.

I push open a sliding glass door.

Chickadee-dee-dee!

Warmth spreads across my chest. I smile as I step out onto the balcony. Drelark is already there, and he's looking toward the birdsong. I join his side, enjoying a comfortable silence as we listen to the wind dance in the trees, the animals cautiously returning to this island of death.

Drelark's hardened shell is glossy and black in the direct sunlight, gleaming and pristine. He's so beautiful, in his alien way. So unlike a human. Seeing him under the unbroken light of day fills me with awe, like I'm seeing something preternatural.

He notices me staring.

A tendril slips between my thighs, teasing its way past my lips.

This is still the only way we can communicate with words. When he's inside me.

I like this better than when he penetrates my ear.

"My spines tingle. I feel it won't be long until he is here," comes his voice inside my head. Then a pause. "I never expected you to think me beautiful," he confesses as he moves his immense form to coil around me.

When he first appeared to me in dream, it was wearing the guise of Leet, a man I had immensely complicated and powerful feelings about. I understand why, and I'm grateful for it, because it pushed me towards resolution.

Could I have ever accepted Leet for who he is without Drelark? Would I have been able to see our relationship as one sided? Exploitative, even?

I don't know. I wouldn't have survived long enough to find out.

He saved me. Offered me the clarity I so desperately need. He soothed my survivor's guilt, my emotional abandonment of my parents and girlfriend. Inside of me, he coaxed out my strength. I now have insight into the minds of men who are the polar opposite of me. Instead of being crushed by the weight of their evil, I can bear it.

Because of him.

"I only want you. As you are." I smile, my eyes crinkling at the edges. The General removed one of my eyes, but it was a blessing. The only good thing that monster did for anyone.

The eye that has grown in to replace it is strange. I'm still adjusting to it, and I don't think it's quite done growing, but the way I see the world now has changed. Scanning the forest, I spot a large bird perched in the distance. Its body glows faintly. I'm not sure if it's heat or energy that I can see now, but it's a colour I never knew existed.

A glimpse of Drelark's vision.

And he's my favourite thing to look at now.

His horned face, his many limbs, his chitinous body. I can see the tiny details reflected inside of me a thousand times over.

I love all of it. My fingers glide along one of his thick forearms, folding into him. There's no doubt about what we're going to do, and I have no fear I might change my mind.

Leet betrayed me in the most inhumane ways imaginable, and once a man gets a taste of sadism, he craves more.

He got into the chopper.

He's on his way.

Nate was, for once, right. Leet didn't just violate me, use me, and send me to an island to get raped, tortured and murdered.

He was ready to cannibalize me. To consume me whole.

There's nothing he can say now to save himself.

"Everything is ready for his arrival. All we need to do now is wait."

I gasp as Drelark's tendril lengthens, becoming more intrusive. Pleasingly intrusive.

"I can handle it for you. Your revenge. I know how

much you hate inflicting suffering, even when it's deserved," Drelark rasps.

His alien hand caresses my chest, digits spiralling across my flesh to fondle. I am as fascinating to him as he is to me. His exploratory touch sends a shiver of pleasure through me.

"I can do it," I reply soundlessly, my eyes fluttering closed. "Killing Leet is *removing* suffering from the world."

Drelark's long, serrated tongue slides along my flesh, tasting me. He finds me delectable.

I don't fear those big fangs as he savours every little flavour of my human hide. Unlike Leet, he would never *literally* eat me.

"It is that and so much more," he responds with a rumbling inner voice, one that I associate with arousal. His and mine, as they become intertwined. The more time we spend together, the more our lives become inextricably linked.

Our selves.

I always thought the idea of a soulmate was bullshit. Two humans have to rely on clumsy language, crude attempts at intimacy. In the end, I always thought it was two distinct individuals trying to find common values and grow trust and respect for each other. A thing vulnerable to betrayal and pain.

With Drelark, it's not like that at all. There's a selfless-ness, an intermingling that cuts through words and actions. We talk in a language that I don't understand, because I don't understand myself. Not as well as he does.

Our souls are one.

We are mates.

He's a part of me.

His cells have become a part of me.

I am no longer Shayde, but someone new.

Something new.

I smile, my fingers trailing down the centre of his abdomen. His external shell is hard, but he can feel my touch somehow. Maybe it's just that he feels it vicariously through my mind. I don't know where I end and he begins.

His prehensile organ responds to my caress. There's a cracking sound, the shell parting as the thick appendage slides against my belly. I whimper with desire. Through my healing, we haven't mated, and now I'm dripping with need.

Leet will arrive soon, but the anticipation only increases my arousal.

"I need to feel you inside me again, Drelark. Before our guest arrives. I can't wait."

"I can't either," he growls, as his finger slips from my cunt and the connection between us is severed. But only for a moment.

My tiny form basks in his shadow as I brace myself with both hands on the polished marble handrail.

He mounts over me. His sleek, long member pierces me in that smaller finger's place. I cry out, forgetting just how large he is. How the swelling stretches me open, and fills me again, heart, soul and body.

We are one like this.

His smaller arms wrap around my chest, still as big as a man's grip. They fondle and grope and hold me close. The larger set of arms bashes against the stonework, holding himself in place as we set out to mate.

It's unnatural. His hips don't piston, they don't need to. His organ pulsates inside me, waves crashing into my cove. It's the most pleasing sensation in the world, his control over his phallus absolute. The moment he senses my will, it moves with dexterity beyond even a human finger. He can articulate every segment of it, and he uses that power to fulfil every fleeting desire I have.

My body is enveloped in his obsidian form, an alien monster claiming his willing damsel.

"I love you," I confess internally. I could never bear to say those words aloud, to face the potential of rejection. With Drelark, knowing it is enough. My feelings swell, my love threatening to engulf me, and instead, it's met with his own emotions.

He doesn't say it; it doesn't come as words. What he feels for me is like love, but unique. Strange. Alien. Like him.

Powerful emotions reach a new intensity, lighting a fire in my mind.

Part of him yearns to rip me apart and ingest me, devour me so that I can be with him forever. I am too precious for him to succumb to the base instinct, though. I've shown him the kindness and trust that was stolen from him, so many decades before.

His view of our love extends into infinity. Beyond the timeframe a human mind can comprehend. Him and I, two separate beings, and yet one, outlasting the Earth, outlasting the stars. Until he and I float in the empty vacuum of space when all reality has crumbled. The last two thinking, rational beings in existence, leaving behind the temporal plane.

I will live in him; he will live in me, even if we are nothing more than stardust.

His member, thick and long and precise in how it works itself inside me, is punctuation to that love.

Four hands are around me. He can explore so much of me at once. The sharp claws are trailed along my soft skin, never threatening to break it. The tendrils explore my breasts, my clit. They suction upon my nipple and clit, the tempo set just as I will it.

Each new penetration enhances our bond. As if creating a new cable connection between our hot, passionate minds.

My wounds have healed, and though I've had to go slow, a diet of fish and berries has helped fill out some of the sallow parts of me. He's noticed every change, no matter how minor, and his curiosity is driven by pure desire.

He wants to know me intimately, more intimately than is possible. It's ironic that the one thing he shares in common with Leet is a dark urge to consume me, but he would never give into that base instinct. He's evolved beyond those impulses, despite being locked away for centuries.

A rush of wind swirls around us and I gasp in delight, buckling forward as Drelark worships my body, inside and out.

That member inside me pulses and thrusts of its own accord. The silvery fluid of his loins flows into me even as we continue to make love.

Whenever his hands leave my breasts, they bounce and jiggle before they're clasped, fondled and appreciated all over again. He pinches my nipples, making them smart, but in that oh so perfect way that is just too hard *enough*.

"We will make our mark on the world," he assures me in the throes of our passion.

I know he's right. It's only been a week, but turns out, Nate was *shit* with cyber security. Taking over his role as the Chief Marketing Officer has been easy.

Soon, the Umbridge Lodge will welcome the newest hunting party who have a taste for human flesh. I will watch Drelark devour them. My lips twitch in a sick smile. The darkness within me grows, but I'm the architect of its development. I nurture it, letting it fill me. A vessel for righteous vengeance.

I shudder, my orgasm broaching.

Drelark knows how to encourage it, to nurse and grow it. Nothing I'd ever experienced before him could compare to the bliss he gives me. Even if I had not fallen for him, come to admire the beauty of his strange form, I could not deny the potency of his cock-like shaft. He wields it with skill beyond what any human man could.

He prods me to that edge, knowing my limits, knowing how to violate those limits in that perfect way that makes my screaming bliss all the more intoxicating.

The connection between our bodies and minds seems to ricochet pleasure back and forth between us. I can feel his physical bliss, and he mine, and they overlay and build on one another until I am unsure if he is penetrating me, or I him, but all at once, and at the same time, and...

Something shatters.

I buckle under the pressure, the way he plays my body with expert skill, plucking his instrument. My orgasm is screaming and bucking, his four arms holding me against his hard shell. Pain and pleasure meet at the border, the line drawn in shifting sand, and him responding to that line with grace and aptitude.

There's another sound, a clatter. I can barely hear it over the haze of ecstasy, but Drelark's spines click rhythmically as they erect in alarm.

Danger.

I feel it, hear it, know it.

Our guest of honour has arrived.

CHAPTER 30

Leet is more beautiful than I remember. I see him in a broader spectrum of light, reflected hundreds of times in my multifaceted eye. A wolf in sheep's clothing. It's no wonder I fell so hard for him.

His new outfit is expensive; bespoke. He's put on weight since I last saw him, and it suits him well. There's a softness to the harsh angles of his face. The wealth he earned by selling me out to rapist cannibal warmongers drapes off of him.

Horror twists his expression. Disgust. Fear.

I can smell it in the air, and it is delicious.

Drelark wraps his biggest arms around me protectively as he lets loose a clattering roar unlike anything meant to be heard by human ears. I am his mate, and he rages with protective fury.

This isn't how I planned on greeting my former crush, but it exceeds anything I could have come up with. A puddle forms at his feet.

His fashionable suit is soiled.

I'm still hazy from my orgasm. We haven't yet uncoupled. Despite Drelark's control over his organ, he can't retract it from me too soon without pain and damage. The knot is tied. We're bound together.

As he turns to tower over Leet, I'm still attached to him. My feet leave the ground, and I float towards Leet. I hover in the air, and Leet cowers at my feet.

"Shayde! I didn't know. I didn't know!"

Connected so intimately, and the hour of my long-needed vengeance at hand, I am in a poor position to exact it. But Drelark won't take it from me.

Instead, he surrenders his body to me.

Those mighty arms, tipped with sword-like claws, are mine.

They move to my impulses alone now.

I twinge with pity. Longing. Though he violated and betrayed me, I can't deny that I once felt love for him. Gratitude. Fascination. For years, I got to know him, and he slowly worked his way past my defenses.

"You didn't know what?"

"What this place is! I just told them that you were snooping around. I had no idea they'd send you away."

"You knew what I was doing could be considered treason."

Tears flood his black eyes, and he grovels, moving towards me before looking at Drelark looming over my shoulder and thinking better of it. His fear turns to confusion, then anger.

"What have they done to you? What is that thing?"

Drelark is quiet in my mind. A silent observer, despite our intimate connection. He relinquished control of his body, because he wants me to make the decision I want to make. I sense his support radiating from him. His angry need for vengeance stilled.

For almost two months, I had endured unthinkable things. To be hunted as game, starved, beaten, tortured. Without Drelark's protection, what I could have endured would have been even worse.

"And it's all because of you," I say out loud, forgetting how humans communicate.

Forgetting that Leet can't feel my pain.

Except... he can.

I can make him feel it.

Drelark's ability goes both ways, after all.

I reach out for him with one of the smaller, less intimidating hands. He shrinks away, but I have the advantage of size for once. The shell cracks open. Before Leet can shrink away, the tendril enters his ear, connecting our minds.

I'M A DECADE YOUNGER, stick thin, stringy black hair. My body hides in a black hoodie. I remember the office I worked at after the asylum. Through Leet's eyes, I watch myself. Memories are imprecise, inexact, but a lot of time passes. I'm working on some code. I don't know anyone is watching me.

This isn't the day we met.

It's months later before he introduces himself with a

shy smile and a soft voice. He's kind, but I'm suspicious. I'm brusque. I don't trust him.

He keeps coming back, asking for me. I'm the only one who can help him with what he needs. The smartest girl he's ever met. Can I please show him how I can code so fast? Where did I learn? Wow, self taught, that's amazing!

A crack in my wall appears. I smile at him. He feels smug satisfaction.

A few weeks later, he has good news. I've been taken off the terrorism watchlist. It was all a misunderstanding. Of course I was just worried about my cousin. Of course I was upset after her death. Yes, I was a minor at the time.

I had my life back.

I looked at him differently then.

He reports to his superiors that his mission will be successful.

He is a poison pill. A spook.

Our meeting was not fate. It was not serendipity. It was cold and calculated, because the best way for him to move up in the company was to protect its assets from people like me.

There were others. There are others. Faces blur into each other, mine becoming just one of a crowd. Time has no meaning in his mind, but some images are fresher than others. He's slept with some of them. Never by force. That was reserved for me.

His first successful target.

He was paid an unthinkable sum of money for me. He didn't need it. It just got added to his investment portfolio. He'd hidden the extent of his wealth from me, lied about the company providing his flat instead of paying him a full salary.

His internal life reminds me of Todd's, of Nate's, but his emotions are stronger. Greed. Envy. Self-pity.

The misogyny is a familiar current. He's laughing at the bar.

"I can't believe it either, man. She offered herself up like a lamb to the slaughter. How deluded was she to think she could take down an arms factory? That place has security up the wazoo, and no way I'm fuckin' up my job for some stuck-up bitch."

The man slaps him on the back. A co-worker, someone Leet loathes, but he wanted to celebrate, so he tolerated him for the night.

"You were playin' a risky game, my man. She could've chickened out and fucked you over."

"Naw, you don't know her. She's like this tortured bird who looks up to me like I'm God just because I handled some watchlist shit for her. Well, the company did, but I got to take credit."

"Some balls on you," the co-worker says, rising a glass in toast. "Did you at least get to hit that before she was sent off to the slaughterhouse?"

Leet laughs. Nods. He's so happy I almost vomit.

"Best part was I could do whatever I wanted to her. What's it gonna matter, right? I knew she'd pull through. Fuck, she'd probably blame herself, carve up her wrists some more. But I'm tellin' ya, man. She *loved* me. Stupid bitch."

I can't take anymore. Any ounce of love I had for this man has been obliterated. I'm gutted, and instead of drawing in his own memories, I reverse the process.

It begins with a trickle. My earliest memories of showing my parents some art I made, and them telling me to focus on a practical skill. They rip it up in front of me. I don't talk about art anymore. Instead, I pretend to read books beyond my age. They are moderately accepting of this, but I should be further ahead. Our neighbour's child is already reading college textbooks.

Disjointed memories of abandonment swirl together. Some are memories. Some are absences of memories. There are no shows of affection, no warmth. Aimi visits, and I tell my parents I wish she was my mom. Aimi leaves, crying. She's still only a teenager, but I want to go with her.

I'm not allowed to talk to her anymore. All that remains is academia. I need to set myself apart so I can get a good job in advanced physics. The world will always need more energy and weapons. I get into Owasis Prep. Eat prat for the first time. My parents smile at me as I eat it and I tell them it's delicious. It makes me sick but I hide it, because my parents are approving of me.

Not proud.

Approving.

I meet someone at school. They have a fantastic style and a sharp tongue. They don't care what people say about us, and tells me my parents suck. When they confide in me they're trans, I help her pick out her new name. Vivian. It's sharp and stabby at the start, but then softens as it rolls from my tongue. She loves it. Loves me.

She's the first one I'm intimate with, and I'm so scared, but so happy. I fantasize about us running away together, out towards Seattle to join the Western Resistance. She tells me we could do more damage from the inside, and I'm excited at the prospect.

I ignore her when she says I should leave well enough alone. Of course, rich kids are given an advantage in the grading system. It's not my business. I should keep my head down and my nose out of it.

The righteousness and foolishness of youth will not let me drop it.

I hack the school, expose the grade tampering. My parents kicked me out. Vivian can't make it work with me anymore, sorry. Aimi...

Leet's eyes roll back into his head, leaving only the whites. He has heard this story before. I've told him all about this, but he has never *felt* it before. Not the way I felt it. Every injury is a stab through my guts. By the time I'm visiting our first meeting, and he's feeling my cautious curiosity, my hopefulness that he'd be back, he's screaming.

"No! Stop! Stop!"

Every moment of our time together that I can remember is pulsed into his head. The emotional current is radioactive, searing into the soft tissue of his brain. His neurons are forced to rewire themselves to understand compassion, love, in a way he could never have known.

"Shayde, it's okay. After this, nothing's going to matter, anyway."

"I'm not on birth control, Leet. Come on, we can do this later. The shop on the main floor has condoms."

He's more forceful, and I stare up at him, begging him to listen. To not reject me. He frowns, thoughtful, and then his mouth is on me. I'm silenced, and he swallows my protests.

We're in the woods now. Our skin is covered like a rash in black fly bites. The hunters are coming.

Leet reaches up, scratching his skin. Angry red gashes line his face. I sway in the air, suspended on Drelark's phallus. Though Leet has lived a lifetime through my mind, it has been only moments in real life. I pass onto him what it was like living on this island. He sees Drelark, and instead of rage and anger, he is forced to feel desire.

He is speed running agony. His entire nervous system is recruited in the effort as it recreates all of my pain and hurt.

"That's it... this is what you have wrought," I tell him.

He's a shell of a man. His black hair bleeds the darkness as I observe, stark white strands taking their place. Lines etch his skin, years added to his life as I force him to live life through my mind.

He coughs up blood.

My stomach growls in response. I release him, and he lay, catatonic, on the balcony. Drelark lowers me to the ground, and with a second of discomfort, we finally decouple.

He caresses my face, and I touch my tongue to one of his tendrils.

"Thank you for that."

Warmth radiates from my mate. He is happy that I've attained what I needed.

"You deserved better. We are the same in many ways. I was feared for things I couldn't control, but you were abandoned, even in the presence of those who should have loved you."

Tears spring to my eyes, and we embrace. Leet whines. Drelark strokes my cheek, pushing away a stray tear.

Something stirs within me. The kindling of something new.

"What do you wish to do now?" Drelark asks, our conversation private, occurring only within our minds.

I regard Leet. His pain has warped his attractive form, his body contorted unnaturally as a pool of waste seeps through his clothes.

"Our child hungers within me."

Something miraculous grows in my womb. Something born of fate. He knows as well as I do what it means, and his alien understanding of love fills the three of us with warmth.

This island, the evil men who wish to hunt for humans, will feed me. Our child. Drelark and I turn on Leet, who has no idea of the role he will play. I am glad that I still feel pity for him. I am not heartless, but I understand now that unyielding compassion is a tool that the wicked wield.

Life leaves him and it is quick. As peaceful as a brain hemorrhage can be. Blood trickles from his ear, dripping onto his carefully tailored suit, and an errant tear escapes my eye. It is shed not for him, but for the girl I was. The girl he killed. I've been reborn, and he was her last connection to the world that will never accept me back.

"Goodbye, Leet. I will remember who you were. Who I wished you were. If not for you, I would not have found my destiny. Your sacrifice will not go to waste."

A short eulogy, but one that he deserves. I am unable to offer him absolution, but knowing that the other girls he was grooming to become prey will be, for now, safe of his threat. And I will not let him go to waste. Something good will come from his body, and his death.

As I take my first bite of human flesh, I do not retch. It is sweet and earthy. Inside me, a soft voice murmurs, communicating with me just as its father does. I cannot yet understand. In time, I will.

Drelark and I have no idea what shape it will take. Only guesses.

Whatever it becomes, we will nurture and shape it as an avatar of justice.

Thank you for reading. Please visit http://jmkeep.com to discover more unique dark fantasy romances. If you enjoyed this novel, you may also like Her Descent and Natural Born Sinners.

Selected Works by J.M. Keep

Novels:

Novellas:

Series:

About the Author

J.M. Keep is the penname of a husband and wife who are already living their happily-ever-after.

Maybe because their real life is so sunny, they love to write dark and twisted tales with morally challenged characters. Most of their stories are dark fantasies where horror and romance are intertwined.

Make sure to sign up for the newsletter for exclusive content, information on new releases, and free books!

facebook.com/jmkeep

instagram.com/jmkeep

bookbub.com/authors/j-e-keep

amazon.com/J.M.-Keep/e/B00DFW3QTM

www.ingramcontent.com/pod-product-compliance
Lightning Source LLC
Chambersburg PA
CBHW020441270626
47155CB00022B/924